I stared at the Flinduvian in horror. . . .

Somehow the alien had figured out that Grampa's spirit was inside my body with me. The weapon he was pointing at my head looked almost like a toy, with a wide mouth at one end and a yellow bottle-like thing at the other. It would have been funny, except that I knew the bottle was meant for collecting souls, and the alien was after Grampa's.

The Flinduvian smiled, his snaky tongue flicking out at me. The big black holes in its tip opened and closed like sniffing nostrils. "Come out, come out, wherever you are!" hissed the alien.

Then he pulled the trigger.

BRUCE COVILLE'S
BOOK OF

Compiled and edited by
Bruce Coville

Assisted by
Lisa Meltzer

Illustrated by
John Pierard

A GLC Book

AN
APPLE
PAPERBACK

SCHOLASTIC INC.
New York Toronto London Auckland Sydney

**For our merry band of writers,
without whom these books would not exist.
Thanks, gang. You've done a great job.**

ISBN 0-590-85296-5

12   11   10   9   8   7   6   5   4   3   2   1   7   8   9/9   0   2/0

Printed in the U.S.A.   40

First Scholastic printing, May 1997

CONTENTS

Contents

INTRODUCTION:

A DIFFERENT KIND OF FEAR

You want to know what's scary? I'll tell you what's scary: starting a serial that is going to appear in five installments, in books that are already scheduled, when you have *no idea how the whole thing is going to end!*

It's a little like jumping out of a plane and hoping you'll be able to finish sewing your parachute before you hit the ground.

On the other hand, writing is always like that to some degree. Even if you think you know where you're going, the story can shift and twist under your fingers so that all of a sudden BANG! there you are, out on a cliff that you never expected to be hanging from.

To tell you the truth, that's not even the scariest part about writing. Here's something else that's scary: You never know if people are going to like what you've done until it's actually

Introduction

out there on the bookstore shelf—which may be months (or even years) after you've written it. And you *do* want to know, because your words are like your babies; they're part of you, and you want people to love them.

If you've been reading all the books in this series of anthologies, it's probably obvious that what's prompting these thoughts is that this volume contains the final part of "The Monsters of Morley Manor."

Now I'll tell you a secret: I started this serial because I couldn't figure out an ending for "Little Monsters," the lead story in my *Book of Monsters II!* Well, that's not quite accurate. I had an ending, and it was okay. But okay isn't good enough. The story felt incomplete to me. So I decided to turn it into a serial—which meant that, for the last year, every two months I have had to come up with a new installment. (And every two months poor Lisa Meltzer, who is my assistant on these books and responsible for getting them to the printer on time, has had to have a near nervous breakdown waiting for me to finish my job.)

To make things even trickier, I had to make the story fit the topics of our different books— which meant I had to figure out a sensible way to add aliens and ghosts to the mix. I can't think of another story that has monsters, aliens, and ghosts all together. Believe me, I muttered and grumbled along the way. ("*What have I gotten myself into?*" I groaned on a regular basis.)

But now that it's all done, I'm glad I did it.

Because I really like the story.

I hope you will, too.

As a matter of fact, I'm terrified that you won't.

Writing. It's a scary business.

Here it is at last—the grand finale.

THE COLDEST TOUCH
(Part 5 of "The Monsters of Morley Manor")

Bruce Coville

What has happened so far:

It all started when I bought a box of monsters and they came to life. The five little monsters begged me and my sister Sarah to return them to their home, creepy old Morley Manor, so they could get big again.

No sooner had we managed *that* than this weird guy called the Wentar showed up and dragged us through a "Starry Door" to get away from some evil aliens called Flinduvians. On the planet where we landed, we learned that the Flinduvians wanted to kidnap Earth's ghosts to use in a weapon.

Our group split up. Some went to spy on the

aliens. Gaspar (the leader of the monsters) brought the rest of us back to Earth. With my grandmother's help, we went to the Land of the Dead to warn the ghosts. Grampa's ghost took advantage of the situation to hitch a ride in my body when we came back.

The other monsters had also returned. But before we had a chance to talk, a group of Flinduvians showed up. They revealed their plan to use Earth's ghosts to reanimate dead Flinduvian warriors. And when they figured out that I had a ghost inside me, one of them came to "collect" Grampa.

I. The Collecting Jar

I stared at the Flinduvian in horror. Somehow he had figured out that Grampa's spirit was inside my body with me. The weapon the alien was pointing at my head looked almost like a toy—colorful and bulgy, with a wide mouth at one end and a yellow bottle-like thing at the other. It would have been funny, except that I knew the bottle was meant for collecting souls, and the alien was after Grampa's.

The Flinduvian smiled, his snaky tongue flicking out at me. The big black holes in its tip opened and closed like sniffing nostrils. "Come out, come out, wherever you are!" hissed the alien.

2

Then he pulled the trigger.

I heard a crackle, and felt a buzz of energy, a little like the feeling we got when we went through the Starry Doors.

Hold on, Grampa! I thought. *Hold on!*

Someone screamed (later I realized it had been me). Then everything went black.

I felt a horrible wrenching, as if I was being pulled apart at the seams. I thought, at first, that it was because Grampa was being ripped from inside me.

It took me a while to realize that the real situation was even worse. It wasn't Grampa who had been ripped out of my body. It was me! *I* was the one who got sucked into the collecting jar!

At first I just felt like I had fainted or something. Then, for a little while, it was as if I was in a dream—the kind where you know you're dreaming, but can't force yourself to wake up. Finally I began to realize where I was.

I screamed again, but it didn't make any difference, since no one could hear me. I suppose it was because I didn't really have a mouth. I didn't have eyes or ears, either, but somehow I could still hear and see what was going on. Don't ask me how that worked. I suppose I was hearing and seeing the same way that ghosts do—the same way I had when we left our bodies to go to the Land of the Dead. I hadn't thought about it as much then, because I was still in a shape that *resembled* my own body, instead of being stuffed in a bottle.

As I began to get a sense of what was going on, I realized that Grampa was putting on a big show.

"How could you just take him like that?" he cried. He was speaking with my voice, through my mouth, and clutching the sides of *my* head.

"What's happening?" cried Gramma. "Anthony, what's going on?"

Grampa turned my body toward her and said, "It was Grampa. He was inside me, and they pulled him out."

A cold fear gripped me. Was he planning to *keep* my body? Was it possible my own grandfather would betray me like that? But why else would he be lying to her?

Gramma was furious. "You let my husband out of that bottle!" she cried, lunging at the Flinduvian. Gaspar caught her and held her back.

The Flinduvian laughed. "I'll let him out when the time is right. Out of the bottle . . . and into the body of a Flinduvian warrior. His life force will animate that body, but control of it will be ours. He will be a perfect slave."

Gramma didn't understand any of that, of course, since she hadn't had a translation spell put on her. But I did, and believe me, it didn't do anything to make me feel better about my situation.

Things got even worse when the Flinduvian yanked the bottle off the end of his gun and dropped it into a pack he was carrying. Everything went dark. I couldn't see or hear at all.

I had just come back from the Land of the Dead. In my opinion, this was far worse.

The only good thing about it was that it gave me a chance to think. In fact, thinking was about the only thing I *could* do under the circumstances. Actually, that's not quite true. I could also *panic*, which was the first thing I did. Not that it did me any good. I mean, usually when you panic you run around and scream, or hyperventilate, or something like that. All I could do was feel like I *wanted* to do that stuff. The feeling kept growing and growing, until I thought I was going to explode. That might not have been all bad. Maybe the bottle would have exploded too—though I don't know if I would have zapped back into my body then, or just been left floating around like a ghost.

A living ghost. What a weird thing to be.

When you panic, you're supposed to take deep breaths. Since I had no nose, mouth, lungs, or air, I couldn't do that. Finally I started to pray. That helped. I didn't get a miracle or anything. But I did settle down, which was sort of a miracle all by itself, if you consider my circumstances.

Then I was able to start thinking. The first thing I needed to think about was why Grampa was pretending to be me. I finally decided he was trying to fake out the aliens. Maybe he figured if they *thought* they had a ghost, but had really gotten the spirit of a living person, there might be some advantage to keeping that fact from them.

At least, I hoped that was what he was thinking. Part of me was afraid what he was really thinking was, "Yippee! I'm alive again!"

The second thing I needed to think about was why the Flinduvian collecting gun had taken me and left Grampa in my body. I came up with two reasons that sort of made sense. The first was that the Flinduvian leader had mentioned that Earth's ghosts have an "absurdly strong" connection to their earthly life. Maybe Grampa, having already experienced death, was clinging to life more tightly than I did. The second possible reason was our recent trip to the Land of the Dead. Since I had already been out of my body, and not that long ago, maybe I hadn't settled back into it properly, wasn't as tightly connected to it as I should have been.

Maybe it was the two things put together.

Well, all that might explain why I had gotten

pulled out of my body. But it didn't tell me what I *really* needed to know—namely, what should I do next? Of course, when you've been yanked out of your body, trapped inside a bottle, and then crammed into an alien's backpack, your options for action are pretty limited.

So is your sense of time. I had no idea how long I had been in the bottle panicking, praying, thinking before one of the Flinduvians pulled the bottle out again.

Holding me up he said, "Let's give this one a try. Bring in one of the corpses and we'll put him inside."

II. I Become a Flinduvian

The Flinduvians carried in a box that looked something like a coffin. It was bigger than most coffins—though given how big the Flinduvians were, that made sense. It was also very plain, with no decorations or fancy woodwork or anything. The only marks on it at all were some squiggles, which might have been Flinduvian writing.

They stood the box on end, then touched a button.

The front swung open.

Inside stood the hulking figure of a dead Flinduvian.

My new home.

Like the other Flinduvians, this guy had muscles on his muscles, tentacles instead of fingers, and feet that looked like long, flexible horse-hoofs. Even though its eyes were closed, you could tell they were big and bulgy. So was its snout.

They carried the collecting bottle over and connected it to a pipe on the side of the box. Then they pumped me inside.

I was plunged into a cold and darkness unlike anything I had ever known before as my spirit was forced into the dead flesh. After a moment I could feel the body coming to life, feel the alien blood pumping through its alien veins. I wanted to scream, but couldn't; the body was not mine to control, merely to inhabit.

My eyes blinked open and I could see again. But seeing the world as a Flinduvian is very different from seeing it as an Earthling. First, colors did not look the same. It wasn't as simple as them looking lighter or darker than usual. They looked like nothing I had ever seen before. It's hard to explain clearly, but I have to tell you, it was pretty freaky.

Second, Flinduvian eyes are much sharper than ours. I could see things I had never seen before: the individual threads of clothing, the flecks of color in the eyes of someone twenty feet away. I could count the hairs on Gaspar's hand.

But along with that sharpness came something that I can only describe as "interpretation." Every object I saw seemed like either a potential danger or a potential weapon; sometimes both at once. And every non-Flinduvian being, even my sweet old grandmother, looked like a menace and an enemy. If it hadn't been for the lucky fact that I had no control over the body I was in, I might have rushed forward to crush her.

I did not like being a Flinduvian. But at least I could see why they were so nasty—though I wondered if they saw things this way *because* they were so nasty, or they were so nasty because of the way they saw things.

The leader of the group took a black box from his pack. He turned a dial and I felt a jolt of power tingle through me.

"There," he said. "He's been activated. Zarax, step forward."

I had no choice. I stepped forward. Must be Zarax was my name.

The leader smiled. "See how simple it is? It takes only moments to reactivate the body with one of your ghosts. Once done, that body is completely under our command."

"What about the ghost itself?" asked Gaspar. "What happens to it?"

The leader's tongue flicked out. "The ghost is merely a battery—a life-force to energize the body. And since the device that prevents more than ten members of a species from passing through a Starry Door on any given day does not apply to dead bodies, we can bring through a million of these corpses if need be. With a small advance group in place to activate them, we can transport an army large enough to conquer this puny planet in a matter of hours."

He stretched his chest triumphantly. "Once the planet is ours, the real work begins. We will harvest your ghosts. Then, using them as fuel for our warrior's bodies, we will take our rightful place as rulers of the galaxy."

I thought about the sorrowful spirits we had met in the Land of the Dead, and imagined them being imprisoned in Flinduvian bodies as I now was. I thought about Grampa being stuck here. I thought about old Mr. Zematoski from across the street who had died last month, and Edon Farrell's big sister, who had been killed in a car accident two years ago. The idea of their spirits being stuffed into these cold Flinduvian corpses was so appalling it made me want to twitch.

To my surprise, one of my new arms did twitch.

What made this surprising was that I was not

supposed to have any control of the Flinduvian body at all.

I tried to do it again.

Nothing.

I focused my thoughts, putting all my energy into moving the right hand.

Nothing . . . nothing . . . nothing . . . *twitch!*

I stopped immediately. I didn't want the Flinduvians to know what I was up to. I tried glancing around to see if any of them had noticed, but twitch or not, I didn't have control of my eyes. All I could do was look straight ahead.

The room was not a pretty sight.

It was, however, a fairly crowded one, despite the fact that all the furniture was gone.

Standing in the parlor of Morley Manor were my sister, my grandmother, and me (or, to be more precise, my body, currently occupied by my grandfather). Surrounding them was the Family Morleskievich: Gaspar and Marie, who had taken on their human forms; Darlene, still in her vampire-woman form; Bob, the family's faithful were-human (Bob was now in his cocker spaniel form); and Albert, Gaspar's hunchbacked assistant—who wasn't a blood member of the family, but might as well have been.

Also standing with them was some version of Gaspar's twin brother, Martin. I say "some version" because though both Martin and Gaspar had been born over ninety years ago, at this point Gaspar was only about forty, and Martin looked to be no more than twelve or so. The thing was, I had no idea if he was the real Martin (who sounded as if he had been kind of a creep, from what I'd heard so far) or one of the clones the Flinduvians had made of him.

And, of course, there were the Flinduvians themselves: eight of them, huge and nasty. They took up a lot of space. I had no idea what to do next. It didn't make any difference. The Flinduvian leader decided for me. Twisting the dial on his control panel, he sent me to stand against the wall.

"Close your eyes and wait for future orders," he ordered.

I did as I was told.

The darkness was complete. I couldn't move. The dead body, though animated by my spirit, was the coldest thing I had ever experienced.

I wanted to shiver, but couldn't, which made me want to scream.

I couldn't do that, either.

It was, I suppose, a lot like being dead.

III. Head Games

My sight was gone. I had nothing to touch or taste. But I did have two working senses: I could hear, and I could smell. As I began to settle into the body I realized it was not only Flinduvian eyes that were sharper than ours. My new nose was much sharper as well. It took me longer to get used to that, simply because I wasn't used to smelling things so clearly. And a lot of what I could smell, I couldn't figure out, because I didn't know how to interpret it.

Still, by listening carefully, and paying attention to the information coming from my snout, I began to associate specific smells with specific people. (Or aliens, or monsters; whatever.) Once I had figured that out, I began to be able to get a sense of where people were standing, and when they moved. After a while I also realized that their odors *changed* when they were talking. I could actually smell fear, anger, and confidence.

As time went on it became clear that the Flinduvians were waiting for some higher officer who was supposed to take charge of the situation.

"Where is Jivaro?" growled the leader two or three times. By tracing his smell I could tell he was pacing back and forth across the floor.

"Who cares? Why don't we just destroy these fools and get it over with?" asked one of the other Flinduvians.

The leader walked over to him. Though the soldier made no sound of pain or protest, from the sound of things I got the impression that he was getting smacked upside the head.

"Because, you moron," roared the leader, when he was done whacking the other guy, "the only one really worth killing is the Wentar, and we can't do that without a higher officer present."

"You'd be wiser not to do it at all," said the Wentar in peaceful tones.

"Shut up, you meddling fool!" screamed the leader.

The anger in his voice was terrifying. Yet he didn't take a step toward the Wentar, or any of the others.

Given how much trouble the Wentar had gotten us into, I was glad to know that he was of some use.

While all this was going on I continued struggling with the body I was in, trying to get control of it. It was hard to tell if I was succeeding, since I didn't dare make any big movements. I couldn't even try opening my eyes, since that would alert them to what I was doing. Mostly I tried clenching my butt muscles. That may sound stupid, but can you figure anything else you can move when it's a matter of life and death that no one in front of you notice the slightest twitch?

I was also sort of exploring the body, trying to get used to it—to its size and its power, its weird differences from a human body. Some of those differences were obvious—the tentacles that I had instead of regular fingers, the weird feet. Some were less obvious—like the incredible strength I now possessed. (The reason that was less obvious was because I had no way of using it.)

As time went on I began to settle more deeply into the body. I figured this was good, because it would make it more likely I could get control of it at some point. But it also made me nervous. What if, in settling in, I got so connected to the body that I could never get out again?

That was a terrifying thought.

It got even more terrifying when I began to find fragments of the previous owner's memories clinging to the brain.

Who knows how the connection of mind and body, spirit and flesh, really works? Not me. So don't ask me to explain this. But it was pretty eerie, let me tell you; as if I wasn't in the body alone. Well, not quite; the previous owner was clearly gone. Yet his memories lingered on, bits and pieces of his life, like the furniture, photos, and knick-knacks left behind in an old house after its owner has died.

The first memory I experienced was as scary as a cold hand grabbing you in a dark room, partly because it seemed to come out of nowhere. I nearly jumped. (Except I couldn't, of course; even so, I did feel my new body flinch a bit.)

The memory was as intense as my best daydreams, and deeply terrifying. The terror came because my immediate reaction was that the alien who had first owned the body was still in it; that I was trapped in this body with its ghost.

"Get me out of here!" I wanted to cry.

If I had been in a room instead of a body I would have beat at the door with my fists, flung myself against it, trying to break it down. But this body had no door.

The memory itself was simple enough: it was of standing on a mountaintop, staring at a city far below. Even though the city was squat and ugly, the view was beautiful. Yet there was no pleasure connected to the memory, only a flash of terrible fear and loneliness. More information bubbled up, and I suddenly understood that the memory was from a childhood day when my body's owner had been abandoned on that mountaintop in order to toughen him up.

Clearly, growing up Flinduvian was not easy.

Other memories began to surface, like bubbles rising in a glass of soda: memories of fear, of being hit, of being trained to be cruel and ferocious. One that still haunts me is of being put in a locked room with three other kids, and only enough water for two of us to make it out alive at the end of the time we were going to be inside.

I can't talk about that one in any more detail. It still upsets me too much.

I almost began to feel sorry for these guys—though that didn't mean I wanted to let them take over the Earth, much less the entire galaxy.

The problem was, how could we stop them?

I certainly didn't expect an answer to my question. I got one anyway. It sounded unexpectedly in my head, seeming to come from nowhere:

"All we have to do is let the Coalition of Civilized Worlds know what they're up to."

This sudden communication was even scarier than the alien memories, and I think I actually did manage to flinch. That was pretty minor, considering that what I *wanted* to do was grab the sides of my head and scream, "Who are you? What are you doing in here?"

I couldn't, of course. But I guess I managed to think it, since the voice answered me.

"This is Martin."

IV. Martin

"Martin?" I thought in astonishment. "As in Gaspar's brother? As in the kid that the Flinduvians brought back with them?"

"No, Martin the next-door neighbor's dog. Of course I'm Gaspar's brother. Now are you going to waste my time with stupid questions, or shall we try to figure out how to solve this mess?"

"You got any suggestions?" I thought, hoping that didn't qualify as another stupid question.

Martin sighed. "Unfortunately, no. But now that I've managed to get in contact with you, at least we'll be in better shape if an opportunity does arise."

That was fine with me. It was the first glimmer of hope I'd had since the Flinduvians showed up. But I was still curious. So despite the crack about stupid questions, I tried another. "I don't get it. Whose side are you on—ours, or the Flinduvians'?"

"My own side," he replied sharply.

"Care to explain that?" I asked.

"Let me check," he said. I didn't feel him go, but I guess he must have, because suddenly he said, "All right, it looks like everything is quiet out there. So let me fill you in on some of the details."

Here's his story. A couple of points I figured out later, but for the most part, this is what he said:

"When I first fell through the worlds into Flinduvia, I was nearly as pleased as I was terrified. At last, it seemed, my quest for greater knowledge of the worlds beyond ours was to be rewarded. Little did I know that the reward would carry with it its own punishment. But that was the case, for in stumbling into Flinduvia, I had entered a place that was as close to a living hell as you will ever find."

Given what little I had learned about Flinduvia from being trapped in the alien body, I had no trouble believing this.

"When I tumbled out of our world, there was a Flinduvian waiting to snatch me up. They had detected the reckless experiments Gaspar and I were conducting, and had created a kind of trap, hoping we would blunder into it.

"It took very little time for them to make a copy of me and send it back to Earth. Not a clone; the clones came later. This was a quick copy job, little more than an animated puppet to hold my place. Within a few days it was replaced by a more sophisticated copy, and a few weeks later another. Finally they had a perfect clone made of me, which they programmed as they wished, then sent off as my final replacement. It studied both my family and our world, sending back information to its masters. But because they had a need to make it believable, the clone had a combination of human and Flinduvian characteristics, which is one reason that it shared some of the great secrets with my family, such as the Starry Doors. The Flinduvians were unhappy about that—partly because if it had been discovered that they had let the secret out to a planet not part of the Coalition of Civilized Worlds the punishment would have been swift and severe. But they felt the risk was worth the possible gain.

"Meanwhile, I was being held prisoner. Or perhaps it would be more accurate to say I was kept as an experimental lab animal. I was poked, prodded and analyzed as completely and impersonally as if I was some important new species of insect they had just discovered—which from their point of view, was pretty much how they saw me.

"Yet after a time, some of them began to talk to me, to tell me about things. I got the feeling they looked on me as we might look on a particularly intelligent pet: someone to share your troubles with. Certainly a Flinduvian would never share his troubles or doubts with another of his own species. That would be seen as weakness, which is the most dangerous trait you can display in their society.

"Now, time in Flinduvia flows differently than it does here, at a ratio of about three to one. That's one reason they were able to send back that first copy in what seemed such a short time to Gaspar: for every minute that passes here, three minutes go by on Flinduvia.

"Which means that I, myself, have lived there for the equivalent of over two hundred and fifty years."

There was such weariness and sorrow in that statement that it nearly broke my heart. But it also confused me. "If you've been there so long, how come you look like you're only twelve?"

"Because this was the body the Flinduvians thought would work best as bait when the Wentar and the others showed up. Besides, even though I have been several different ages, physically speaking, during my time on Flinduvia they liked keeping me as they had first captured me. I think I was a symbol of their first step toward the conquest they dreamed of.

"Anyway, as the years rolled on, as the first century moved into the second, I earned more and more privileges from the scientists who guarded and studied me. One of those was the ability to occasionally don other versions of my body. I could be myself as I would appear at twenty, or thirty, or forty, and so on. There were dozens of copies of me in their lab, and with their technology it was not that hard to move from one to another.

"Which is how I was able to come back to Earth when I discovered that they had called home the clone that had been taking my place here. They knew I hated being in the old-man version of my self, so they didn't put many safeguards on those particular bodies. Late one night I slipped into one of them, then through the Starry Door that leads to the upstairs of this house. That was when I showed your sister the box where my clone had long ago placed my frozen, shrunken family.

"I knew what they had done to Gaspar and the others because they had told me about it when it happened. Flinduvians have no family bonds at all, and since they knew I had had many conflicts with my brother and sisters, they simply assumed it wouldn't make that much difference to me."

His voice grew scornful. "They did not understand the ties that hold together the Family Morleskievich. Blinded by their own cruelty, they could never understand the bond of blood and loyalty I shared with my brother and sisters, no matter how much I might have fought with them. They could never begin to realize how deeply I wanted them set free."

He was silent for a moment, and I got a sense he was brooding about his centuries on Flinduvia. I tried to put myself in his place, imagine what it was like, but the idea gave me cold shivers.

Finally he spoke again:

"Now, here's what you need to know, Anthony. The key to the entire Flinduvian plan is secrecy. If word of what they're up to gets back to the High Council of the Coalition of Civilized Worlds, the Coalition's massed forces will clamp down on the Flinduvians faster than a mousetrap snapping shut. The Council is already suspicious. But this is High Diplomacy, and there are delicate rules to be followed. To have any chance of success, the Flinduvians must have their conquest well under way before anyone realizes what is going on.

"So all we really need to do is break up this situation long enough for the Wentar to get back to his home world and pass on this information. It would be nice if we got out of it alive, too. But given what's at stake, that's really a side issue."

"Are you telling me that the fate of the civilized galaxy rests in our hands?" I asked.

"I'd say that's a fair statement of the situation. But then—wait! Let's listen."

A small argument had broken out among the Flinduvians. Actually, their regular conversations could be considered small arguments, so this was something bigger.

"We should not wait for Jivaro!" shouted one of the warriors, one who had not spoken before. "Let's kill them now and be done with it."

"Who is in command here, Frax?" shouted the leader.

"The question is, who *should* be in command?" replied Frax, giving the leader a shove.

Martin must have sensed my astonishment that a soldier would shove his leader, because he said, "They're like this all the time. A position of power is yours for no longer than you can hold it. They shift—uh-oh!"

Frax, getting louder and angrier, had shoved his way past the leader. "We'll start with the old one," he said. "Just for fun."

I could smell him moving toward my grandmother. In vain, I ordered my body to move, struggling desperately to lift an arm, take a step. No luck. I stood as if frozen.

My little sister had no such problem. "You leave my Gramma alone!" Sarah screamed. I could smell her fear—and her anger, which was at least as strong. I smelled her leaping over to stand in front of my grandmother.

"You'll do just as well for starters!" roared Frax, snatching her off the floor.

Sarah screamed again, this time in pure terror.

V. The Heat of Battle

That was it. I saw a flash of red. Sarah might be a total pain-in-the-butt sister, but she was my pain in the butt, and I didn't intend to let any stinking alien turn her into sister sushi.

"You let her go, you damn Flinduvian!" I screamed.

At the same time my eyes snapped open. I could feel myself taking control of the body at last. Bellowing with rage, I charged forward.

"Zarax, stop!" commanded the leader of the group.

Duh. Like I was going to stop just because he told me to.

He fiddled with the control box, turning the knob, shaking it, shaking it harder, finally flinging it to the floor so hard it burst into pieces.

I reached out with my fist and smashed him in the face as I went past. He hit the floor with a thud.

The alien who had picked up Sarah looked at me in fear and astonishment.

"You . . . put . . . her . . . *down!*" I roared, the words coming out in the harsh language of Flinduvia.

He dropped her. Immediately Darlene and Marie swooped in and snatched her away from the edge of the battle.

And a battle it was. The alien I had challenged had started to pummel me. I didn't care. I was fighting back in a red rage, roaring and shrieking.

Two other aliens jumped me from behind. I

tried to shake them off, but they clamped on to me and dragged me to the floor.

Then, suddenly, complete chaos erupted in the room. It took me a moment to realize what had happened. Gaspar, sensing the moment was right, did what he had not been able to before. Digging in his pocket, he pulled out the "distraction" device the Wentar had given him before we left for the Land of the Dead.

It exploded in a cloud of smoke that gave off bright flashes of color. As each flash burst, it emitted a high squeal that seemed to go right through my head. It must have been pitched to some note that was particularly excruciating to the Flinduvians, because all of them (me included) slammed their hands to their ears and began to howl.

The humans in the room looked at us in astonishment, as if they couldn't figure out what we were doing.

The pain was incredible, so intense and debilitating that I suspect it came from more than just the sound. But Flinduvian warriors are trained to ignore pain. So the device proved to be no more than what the Wentar had said it would be: a distraction.

The other aliens were the first to move against it. Staggering, groaning, they began to lurch toward the device, with the intention of breaking it, I suppose.

I wasn't used to dealing with such pain. I wasn't used to maneuvering this body. But I had one thing in my favor. The Flinduvians were mere soldiers. I was a brother, a grandson, a friend. They were fighting because it was what they did. I was fighting because I had to save people I loved.

I had one more thing in my favor. This wasn't my body, and I didn't care what happened to it. With a roar I threw myself forward, heading for the device myself.

The pain was phenomenal, pulsing through my skull like razors of fire coated in acid. I pushed through it, screaming and howling in a voice that scared even me. It was like walking through molasses, pushing yourself upstream through a flood of agony. Each of the aliens was moving slowly toward the device. I had to get there first, to keep the advantage.

I pushed ahead, pushed faster.

"Zarax, I command you to stop!" screamed the leader, who was crawling across the floor.

Frax, the soldier who had been arguing with him, stepped on his head—a gesture of contempt for his failure, I guess.

One of the aliens grabbed my arm. I spun and slammed him so viciously it sent him sprawling across the room. Astonished at my own strength, I forged onward. I was about to snatch the device from the floor, turn it toward the others, drive them out of the room, when two of them tackled me. I hit the floor with a crash that shook the walls.

All the Flinduvians were roaring and screaming.

The smell of their rage, fear, and hate burned in my alien nostrils, filling the *real* me with horror. Yet at the same time it seemed to give added power to the alien body.

A blood-red haze clouded my vision. With a roar, I picked up one of the Flinduvians who had tackled me and smashed him against the other. Both fell unconscious.

I started crawling toward the device again. The closer I got to it, the more I felt like my head was going to explode.

So what if it explodes, I told myself through the blazing pain. *It's not your head! Keep going! KEEP GOING!*

I grabbed the device, then staggered to my feet. With the device pointed at the Flinduvians, I began to herd them together at one side of the room.

"Well done!" cried Martin.

I glanced over my shoulder. Marie, Sarah, and my grandmother were gone, which I was grateful for. However, my own body, with my grandfather still in it, was standing wide-eyed, watching what happened. I wished Grampa had taken my flesh and blood somewhere safe.

Gaspar, the Wentar, Albert, and Bob were still there, as well, looking as if they wanted to help, but weren't sure how. Darlene, in her bat form, fluttered above them.

"Watch out!" cried Grampa.

I turned, just in time to see one of the Flinduvians lunging toward me. I kicked forward savagely, catching him in the jaw and sending him reeling back against the wall. I was astonished, and appalled, at my own viciousness.

"Enough," said the Wentar, stepping forward. "It is finished."

Gently, he took the device from my hands.

Pain overwhelmed me, and I collapsed to the floor, blackness swirling around me.

VI. *The Warmest Touch*

When I opened my eyes, my friends and family were staring down at me.

I did a quick check. I was still in the Flinduvian body.

"Horace, are you all right?" asked Gramma.

"That's not Horace, my darling," said my grandfather, who was standing next to her, wrapped in my body. "It's Anthony."

"Then who are you?" cried Sarah, looking at him nervously.

"I'm your grandfather," he said.

Sarah's eyes got wide. "This is too weird," said Gramma.

"I'm sorry, Ethel," said Grampa. "When those monsters snatched away Anthony instead of me, it seemed best not to say anything. I figured what they didn't know wouldn't hurt them."

"It was a wise choice," said the Wentar. "I suspect that the reason Anthony was able to seize control of the Flinduvian body was that he is a living spirit, not a dead one. Your silence may have provided the element of surprise we needed to overcome them."

"So you weren't planning to keep my body?" I asked.

"Of course not!" said Grampa. He sounded indignant, but my face had just enough of a blush on it that I suspected the idea had crossed his mind. Oh, well. If the situation was reversed, I probably would have considered it, too. It's what you do that counts, not what you think about doing, thank goodness.

"So how do we get me out of this thing?" I asked, looking down at my horrible alien body.

"I'm not sure," said the Wentar, sounding uncomfortable.

"Perhaps we could use the Flinduvian collecting gun," suggested Gaspar. "It put him in there; shouldn't it be able to pull him out?"

"It's worth a try," said the Wentar, his long face looking gloomy.

"What happened to the Flinduvians?" I asked. My head was still throbbing, and it was hard to concentrate.

"The group that vas here has been hauled avay," said Darlene, sounding very satisfied.

"Once I had proof of their plans, it was easy to get the Coalition of Civilized Worlds to slap a quarantine on their planet," said the Wentar. "I had long suspected that they were up to something, but it was impossible for us to act without proof. They won't be a menace for a long time again."

"Here's the gun," said Albert, clumping back over to join us. "Who wants to try?"

"I will," said Martin. "I know their technology best."

He pointed the collecting gun at my head. I flinched. On the other hand the pain was so intense that I couldn't wait to get out of the body.

"Ready?" he asked.

I nodded.

He pulled the trigger. A surge of energy surrounded me. Everything went black.

When I opened my eyes, I was still in the Flinduvian body.

"What happened?" I cried in horror.

"Nothing," whispered Marie's snakes, drooping around her head as if in sorrow. "Nothing at all."

"I suspect I know the source of the problem," said the Wentar. "When Anthony went into that berserker rage he meshed himself with the body in a deep way. He was not merely inhabiting it then, not merely providing it with energy. He was *living* in it in the way that it was accustomed to. Now, it doesn't want to let go of him."

I moaned. "Does that mean I have to spend the rest of my life as a Flinduvian?"

No one answered. No one looked happy.

"Maybe I could take his place?" suggested Grampa.

Gramma gasped, but didn't say anything.

"It might work," said the Wentar. "But it would be a bad idea. If I'm correct, and the reason Anthony could seize control of the body is that his spirit was still a living one, you would have no such advantage. It is more likely you would end up a mindless slave, as the Flinduvians had intended."

"Oh, that's all right," said Grampa. "I was married for nearly fifty years."

"Horace!" cried Gramma in shocked tones.

"Just joking," he said softly, and I could tell that the point of the joke was to hold back his horror at what he might have to do to free me.

"I think I have a better idea," said Martin.

33

"I will take over the body. I am already used to switching bodies, since the Flinduvians moved me from clone to clone more times than I can count."

The others started to question him, but he raised his hands. Turning to the Wentar he said, "It would be a good idea, would it not, to have a spy among the Flinduvians—someone who could pass undetected?"

"I suspect it would," said the Wentar. "They will not take this defeat lightly."

"Then it might as well be me."

Darlene started to cry. Martin actually smiled. "Don't be sad, sister dearest," he said gently. "I have been too long gone from this world ever to fit here again. Horrible as Flinduvia is, I belong there now. As I told you while Anthony was sleeping, it's been over two centuries by their time—twenty times as long as I lived on this world. Besides," he said, smiling wickedly, "I have some scores to settle back there."

And so it was decided.

It wasn't easy. Martin came into the body with me, and slowly, bit by bit, replaced my spirit with his. It took hours—the longest, most painful and horrifying hours I had ever known. When he was finally done, we said in one voice, "All right, try the gun again."

The Wentar pointed it at our head and pulled the trigger. Once more the energy engulfed me.

But this time it was different; I could feel myself being wrenched from the body, pulled back into the collecting jar. My panic was brief. It was a matter of but moments to put me back in my own body.

Welcome home, Anthony, said my grandfather. His voice was kind, gentle, and just a little bit sad. *You did a good job, kiddo.*

Then he disappeared from my body. I saw his shape floating before me for just an instant.

He drifted over to my grandmother. Stroking her cheek, he whispered, "I love you so, my darling. Be happy. When the time is right, I'll see you on the other side."

She reached toward him, her hand trembling.

He shook his head sadly, gave her a wink, then faded out of sight.

Before I could react to that, Martin lumbered to his feet—his new Flinduvian feet. He crossed to Gaspar, put his enormous, multi-tentacled hands on his shoulders.

"You are my little brother and my big brother," he said in his new voice. "Our lives have been pulled far apart, farther than ever brothers' lives should be. We are too different now—yet in deep and powerful ways we will always be the same. Though I cannot stay, you will always be part of me."

Then he took Gaspar in his arms and embraced him.

After embracing his sisters, too, he came to me. Wrapping my hand in his tentacles he said solemnly, "It was a pleasure to share a body with you. You have strength and courage."

A moment later he and the Wentar were gone, the Wentar muttering about all the work they still had to do to save the galaxy.

That was the last I ever saw of them.

It was not, however, the last we saw of the monsters. Though Darlene and Marie spend most of their time in Zentarazna these days, they are often guests at Morley Manor, which Gaspar and Albert are restoring to its former glory.

Sarah and I are frequent guests there, too, along with our grandmother.

Mom and Dad don't quite understand what it's all about. That's all right. As I tell them almost every day, "The world is too vast and strange for any of us to understand all of it."

But sometimes, late at night, when I am working with Gaspar in his bizarre laboratory, with its mad mix of magic and science, I think I want to try.

I don't suppose I'll ever manage to know it all. On the other hand, I know a few more things than I used to. Like, what it means to have a family that loves you.

We should all have such warmth.

Sometimes we terrify ourselves, letting our imaginations conjure up monsters and menace. What's really awful is when the world turns out to be even scarier than we imagined. . . .

THE RAGMORE BEAST

Robert J. Harris

Ricky was running for his life, but all he could think of was that his underpants were riding up. He could hardly believe that even in the midst of sheer terror there was a part of his mind that could take the time to be bothered about such a thing.

Can't reach back to pull them loose, he thought. *Got to keep my arms pumping.*

He had to give himself that extra fraction of speed that could be the difference between life and death. He couldn't let anything distract him from the thought of the Beast that was at his heels or he would be done for.

Fast, he thought. *Got to keep going fast.*

He skipped over a tree root, then ducked his head to avoid a low branch. He felt it scraping over the top of his head, briefly snagging a stray curl.

He couldn't hear the Beast now. Maybe he should risk a glance back to see if it had given up the chase. Then he heard the crack of a branch and the sound of underbrush being trampled. And all of a sudden he realized how slow he was going, like a runner in a movie trapped in slow motion so you could watch his face twisting, trace the beads of sweat sliding down his cheeks, hear his breath coming in long ragged pants, every stride taking forever.

Faster before one powerful leap brings it upon you. Faster, before its claws rake your back.

Ricky could almost smell the breath of the thing now, thick with the stink of dead game and dried animal blood, thirsting for the rich taste of human flesh. Did the smell of his sweat make him easier to track? Then his own fear was helping to get him killed.

If he'd had the sense to get properly scared this morning when the whole thing had begun, he wouldn't be in this fix now. If he hadn't let Geoff and Leno talk him into it . . .

"It's probably a big cat," Geoff said. "Maybe a bear."

"Not even a bear's big enough to drag off old man Johnson's prize bull like this thing did. I say it's some new animal that's just come out of hiding. What do you think, Rickster?"

"I don't know," Ricky had answered, kicking at one of the stones that littered Leno's bare front yard. "A few people say they've seen something strange in the woods, but nobody's proved there's anything really out there."

"You hear that?" Geoff said. "Ricky doesn't think there's anything there."

"I never said that," Ricky protested weakly.

Leno clapped him on the shoulder in that fake friendly way he had. "Oh, it's there all right. Me and Geoff are pretty sure of that. And you're going to help us prove it, aren't you Rickster?"

Ricky shook his shoulder free and stepped away from the two older boys. "Help you?"

"Sure," Leno insisted. "The whole town's talking about this beast out in Ragmore Wood, and anybody that can get a picture of it can name his own price. Maybe even sell it to a real paper like *The Washington Post*."

"*National Enquirer*," Geoff suggested. "They'd be more interested in something like this. I don't think it's a regular animal at all."

"Nobody's ever seen it in the daytime," Leno continued, "so I figure it's hiding in those caves out by Keegan's Rock. We're heading out there tonight with a bag full of guts and stuff I got from old man Thomassen's butcher shop. We'll use that to lay a trail that'll lead it to a spot where we can take a picture. While it's busy enjoying its snack, we'll snap our shot and be gone before it's had time to burp. That's where you come in, Rickster."

"Unless you're too scared," Geoff added with a sneer.

"Of course I'm not scared," Ricky told them. "I'll come along."

The only thing he was really scared of at that moment was what the other two boys would think of him. Not that he actually liked them. They were three or four years older and treated him like a flunky half the time. But the only other kids in the neighborhood were practically babies, so it was either hang around with those two or stay at home being ordered about by his parents.

Leno told him where and when to meet them. When Ricky was sure his parents were asleep, he climbed out his bedroom window and hurried to the ruined shack at the edge of Ragmore Wood. Geoff and Leno grinned when they saw him, and Leno gave him a wink before leading the way into the forest.

As soon as the lights of town had disappeared behind the wall of trees, Ricky felt a strong impulse to turn back, to claim he was sick or that he'd just remembered some life-or-death errand back home. But the thought of the older boys laughing at him was enough to push him on.

"This seems like a good place," Leno announced after they'd walked for what felt like a couple of miles. They were standing in a clearing where a circle of elms leered down at them suspiciously. Ricky didn't recognize the spot. Leno looped a camera around Ricky's neck by its strap. "You squat down in those bushes over there, Rickster. Geoff and me'll head over to Keegan's Rock and lay a trail down here. You ready, G-man?"

Geoff hoisted the plastic bag from the butcher's in reply and the two started off.

"If we come back running," Geoff called back, "make sure you get a picture of whatever's chasing us!"

Their laughter was the last thing Ricky heard as they disappeared into the darkness.

An hour went by, and Geoff and Leno didn't come back. Ricky crawled out from the bushes, his back and legs stiff from waiting. Where were those guys? Had they gotten lost? Or had something worse happened? If there really was a beast and they'd gone strolling up to its lair carrying a bag full of bait, wasn't there a good chance it had caught them before they could start laying a trail?

After a while he couldn't wait any longer. Better to go and find out what had happened than hang around here letting his fears get worse and worse. He set out the way he had seen the two older boys go.

A half hour of searching yielded no sign of Geoff and Leno. And no sign of Keegan's Rock. You couldn't miss that rock, for Pete's sake! It looked like some drunk had tried to carve a twenty-foot-high statue of Dick Tracy's nose, then punched a hole through the middle of it. So where was it? Was he in a completely different part of the woods than he knew? He wished he'd paid more attention on the way in.

"Hey, you guys!" Ricky shouted. "Are you there?"

No answer came from the darkness.

His stomach clenched and he chewed his lip. Geoff and Leno were gone—dead for all he knew—and he was completely lost and alone in this dark, gloomy forest. Surely Keegan's Rock or some other landmark must be visible in the dim moonlight. As he whirled desperately around, trying to make out some familiar sight, the camera, hanging by its strap around his neck, struck the trunk of a tree and broke open.

Ricky cursed the added stroke of bad luck. Now if he ever did find Leno he'd be in a world of trouble for breaking his lousy camera! He lifted it in both hands to see if the hinge was still intact when he saw to his surprise that the camera was empty.

His face screwed up as he tried to figure it out. Could they really have forgotten to put the film in? How could they be so dumb when there was something as important as getting a picture of the Beast at stake?

It was then that the truth struck him.

There was no film because there was no beast. The whole thing was a gag, and he'd fallen for it like a complete jerk. They'd brought him out here to the middle of nowhere and left him standing around like a dope, cold and afraid, wondering if some imaginary beast had carried them off, when all the time they were back home, probably loafing in front of the TV, laughing their heads off at the joke.

Angry at himself as much as at them, Ricky pulled the camera off and threw it down.

It hit a rock with a loud crack and smashed into a couple of pieces. But that didn't make him feel any better. He still had to find his way home, and even then all that was waiting for him was laughter. And his parents would probably ground him, too.

Ricky was sinking to the forest floor when a noise off to his right made him jump. He peered through the trees, but at first couldn't see anything. Then he spotted it about twenty yards away, half hidden in the shadows, a dark, hulking shape crashing through the bushes and trees.

It was too dark to make out what it was, but it was growling like a bear or a mountain lion. Ricky's mouth went dry. He started to back away as quietly as he could. Then he saw that the thing was coming his way, picking up speed as it moved.

Ricky took off like somebody had set fire to his rear end.

So here he was now, running like he'd never run in his life. He had no idea where he was in the Ragmore Wood. His one slim hope of safety was to outdistance the Beast long enough to stumble upon a road or a farm.

Ahead was a rippling sound. Yeah, he remembered there being a stream. That was it. Maybe the Beast would lose his trail in the water. He could just make out the faint sheen to his left. He swerved and charged straight for it till he was ankle deep in water, sloshing downstream for all he was worth.

Follow the stream and it won't know where you've come out.

Then he felt just how heavy a drag the water was on his legs. The thing would be on him in another couple of seconds if he stayed in the open like that. Ricky jumped onto the far bank and started running again. But the bottoms of his jeans were so wet it felt as if someone had tied a couple of barbells to his ankles. His sneakers were squelching, the soles so slick with water he could barely keep his footing on the stony shore.

Stupid, stupid, stupid!

He had to hurry, but his chest felt like an overstretched balloon. He knew he couldn't keep this up much longer. It was like somebody was twisting a knife in his ribs, scraping sandpaper over his lungs, melting his bones into Jell-O.

He could barely see the woodland ahead through the darkness and his tears. The only sound he could hear was his own ragged breath. The Beast could be right on top of him, and he wouldn't even know it till it got him.

Then, to his shock, he was falling—twisting and clawing at the air for something to grab on to. He fell six feet to the bottom of a ditch and landed flat on his back. The impact whacked the last whisper of air out of his lungs.

Tears of pain had blinded him to the danger at his feet, and now he knew he was doomed as surely as if the Beast itself had set this as a trap. For all he knew, it had. Who knew what it was, really?

He could hear it coming, its rasping growl

growing louder. Any second it would be upon him.

He heard a voice cry, "Watch out for that ditch, man!"

Then he saw Geoff and Leno leap through the air above him, heard them land on the other side of the ditch and run on for a few yards before stopping.

"Where is he?" gasped Leno.

"I guess he outran us," Geoff answered, gulping in air. "He's a fast little squirt. He's probably wet himself ten times over by now."

They both laughed.

Those jerks! It was them! It had been them the whole time. They hadn't gone home at all. Instead they'd hidden in the underbrush and waited for him to come looking for them so that they could play an even bigger joke on him.

"Growl for me, G-man!" Leno said.

Ricky heard again that same feral sound that had made him take to his heels.

Leno hooted. "That's terrific! You're a regular wolf man!"

"Come on, let's go home and get something to eat."

"Yeah, it's hard work being a beast. The squirt can find his own way home. If he isn't scared to death already!"

The older boys broke into uncontrollable

laughter as they walked away. Listening to them, Ricky felt all his fear and humiliation boil into a blazing rage. His fingers curled into tight fists. He wanted to punch them, kick them, anything to let them know that they were never going to play him for a sap again. He didn't care if they beat him to a pulp, just as long as he could land even one good blow.

With a painful effort he dragged himself upright. He tried to climb the wall, but his wet sneakers kept sliding down, and his fingers were having trouble getting a good grip on the earthen walls. He took a deep breath and tried again. Slowly he made his way up. He was almost at the top when he heard something coming from behind him.

He froze.

A great black shape, its sleek jet fur rippling with muscles, launched itself across the dark expanse above Ricky's head. For a split second Ricky glimpsed the ferocious face of a huge, unearthly hunting cat, its lips curled back to expose two rows of wickedly hooked teeth, its narrowed eyes flashing a merciless green. Then it thudded down on the other side of the ditch. Ricky pulled himself up in time to see the thing bounding after its prey, great paws battering the earth, roaring like a wind out of hell. It was nearly twice the size of any of the lions he'd seen at the zoo. He couldn't believe anything so big could move so fast.

The camera might be broken and empty, but the picture of what happened next would stay with him forever. *The Beast is real,* he thought numbly. *The Beast was not a joke.*

The two older boys turned just in time to scream their lungs out before the creature was on them, its razor-sharp claws lashing out, its slavering jaws gaping wide. Both of them went down at once, their terrified cries cut short as the Beast ripped and tore at them.

Ricky's insides turned to ice and his fingers slipped. He slid to the bottom of the ditch and lay there, his whole body trembling with horror.

A low growl echoed from above, and then he heard the sound of something being dragged off. When that noise had faded, there was only the thunderous hammering of his own heart.

People who try to stay on the cutting edge of fashion know that sometimes the world just moves too fast.

SAME TIME NEXT YEAR

Neal Shusterman

In a vast universe, toward the edge of a spinning galaxy, on a small blue planet flying around the sun, in a place called Northern California, lives a girl who is quite certain that the entire universe revolves around her. Or at least she acts that way. In fact, if an award were given out for acting superior, Marla Nixbok would win that award.

"I was born a hundred years too early," she often tells her friends. "I ought to be living in a future time where I wouldn't be surrounded by such dweebs."

To prove that she is ahead of her time, Marla always wears next year's fashions and hairstyles that seem just a bit too weird for today. In a college town known for being on the cutting edge of everything, Marla is quite simply the Queen of Fads at Palo Alto Junior High. Nothing and nobody is good enough for her, and for that reason alone, everyone wants to be her friend.

Except for the new kid, Buford, who couldn't care less.

Buford and Marla meet on the school bus. It's his first day. As fate would have it, the seat next to Marla is the only free seat on the bus.

The second he sits down, Marla's nose tilts up, and she begins her usual grading process of new kids.

"Your hair is way greasy," she says. "Your clothes look like something out of the fifties, and in general, you look like a Neanderthal."

Several girls behind them laugh.

"All else considered, I give you an F as a human being."

He just smiles, not caring about Marla's grade. "Hi, I'm Buford," he says, ignoring how the girls start laughing again. "But you can call me Ford. Ford Planct."

Ford, thinks Marla. She actually likes the name, against her best instincts. "Okay, F-plus—but just because you got rid of the 'Bu' and called yourself 'Ford.'"

"Didn't you move into the old Wilmington place?" asks a kid in front of them.

"Yeah," says Buford.

51

The kid snickers. "Sucker!"

"Why? What's wrong with the place?" asks Ford, innocently.

"Nothing," says Marla, "except for the fact that it used to belong to old Dr. Wilmington, the creepiest professor Stanford University ever had."

Ford leans in closer to listen.

"One day," says Marla, "about seven years ago, Wilmington went into the house . . . and never came out." Then she whispers, "No one ever found his body."

Ford nods, not showing a bit of fear.

"Personally," says Marla, trying to get a rise out of him, "I think he was killed by an ax murderer or something, and he's buried in the basement."

But Ford only smiles. "I wouldn't be surprised," he says. "There's a whole lot of weird things down in our basement."

Marla perks up. "Oh yeah? What sort of things?"

"Experimental things, I guess. Gadgets and stuff. Does anyone know what sort of research this Professor Wilmington was doing when he disappeared?"

No one on the bus responds.

Ford smiles, and then stares straight at Marla. "By the way," he says, pointing to her purple-tinted hair and neon eye shadow, "you've got to be the weirdest-looking human being I've ever seen."

Marla softens just a bit. "Why, thank you, Ford!"

Marla peers out of her window that night. Through the dense oak trees she can see the old Wilmington house farther down the street. A light is on in an upstairs window. She wonders if it's Ford's room.

Like Marla, Ford is trapped out of his time, only *he* belongs in the past, and she belongs in the future. It's not as if she likes him or anything. How could she like him—he is a full geek-o-rama nausea-fest. But she can use him. She can use him to get a look at all those dark, mysterious machines in his basement.

Marla smiles at the thought. Using people is a way of life for her.

And so the very next afternoon, Marla fights a blustery wind to get to Ford's house. By the time she arrives, her punked-out hair looks even worse, for the wind has stood every strand on end. She likes it even better now.

"Thanks for coming over to help me study," says Ford as he lets her in. "I mean, moving in the middle of the school year sure makes it hard to catch up."

"Well, that's just the kind of person I am,"

says Marla. "Anything I can do to help a friend."

Marla looks around. The furniture is so tacky, it makes her want to gag. The living-room sofa is encased in a plastic slipcover. Ford's mother vacuums the carpet wearing a polka-dot dress, like in "I Love Lucy." For Marla, it's worse than being in a room filled with snakes.

"It's noisy here," says Ford. "Let's go study in my room."

Marla shudders. Who knows what terrors she'll find there?

"How about the basement?" she asks.

"It's creepy down there," says Ford.

"You're not scared, are you?"

"Who, me? Naw."

Marla gently takes his hand. "C'mon, Ford . . . we need a nice quiet place to study."

Ford, who has taken great pains not to be affected by the things Marla says or does, finally loses the battle. He takes one look at her hand holding his and begins to blush through his freckles. "Oh, all right."

While the rest of the house has been re-painted and renovated, the basement has not changed since the day Wilmington disappeared. All of the old man's bizarre stuff is down there. Maybe Wilmington himself is down there somewhere, just a dried-out old skeleton lurking behind a heavy machine. What if they were to find him? How cool would that be?

As they descend the rickety stairs, Marla grips Ford's hand tightly, not even realizing she is doing so. Ford's blush deepens.

"Gosh, I thought you didn't even like me," says Ford.

Marla ignores him, blocking out the thought, and looks around. "What is all this stuff?"

"That's what I've been trying to figure out."

Everything is shrouded in sheets and plastic tarps. Strange shapes bulge out. They look like ghosts, lit by the flickering fluorescent light. There is a warped wooden table in the middle of it all. Ford drops his school books down on the table and a cloud of dust rises. It smells like death down there—all damp and moldy. The walls are covered with peeling moss, and they ooze with moisture.

"We can study here," says Ford, patting the table. But Marla is already pulling the sheets off the machines.

Whoosh! A sheet flutters off with an explosion of dust, revealing a dark, metallic, multi-armed thing that looks like some ancient torture device.

"I wouldn't touch that," says Ford.

Marla crooks her finger, beckoning him closer. Her nails are painted neon pink and blue with tiny rhinestones in the center of each one. She leans over and whispers in Ford's ear, "If you really want to be my friend, you'll help me uncover all these machines."

Ford, his blush turning even deeper, begins to rip off the sheets.

When they're done, a cloud of dust hangs in the air like fog over a swamp, and the machines within that dusty swamp appear like hunched monsters ready to pounce. All they need is someone to plug them in.

Ford sits at the table and studies the old professor's notes and lab reports. But Marla is studying something else—the knobs and switches on the grotesque and fantastic devices are what grab her attention. They might not find Wilmington's body down there, but Marla is happy. This is already more interesting than anything she has done in quite a while.

She joins Ford at the scarred table, going through the professor's old notes page by page.

Hyperbolic Relativistic Projection.

Metalinear Amplitude Differentials.

It makes little sense to them, and Ford has to keep looking things up in a dictionary.

At last, with the help of the professor's notes, they're able to figure out what most of these machines are supposed to do.

The one with a metallic eyeball looking

down from a tall stalk is a waterless shower that can dissolve dirt from your skin by sonic vibrations. But according to Wilmington's footnote, it doesn't work; it dissolves your skin, instead of the dirt.

The device with iron tentacles growing from a steel pyramid is supposed to turn molecular vibrations into electricity. It works, but unfortunately it also electrocutes anyone who happens to be standing within five feet of it.

Another device—a hydrogen-powered engine—was supposed to revolutionize the automotive industry. According to a letter the professor received from the chairman of one of the big car companies, the engine nearly blew up half the plant when they turned it on.

In fact, none of the things Wilmington made worked properly. Not the refractive laser chain saw, or the lead-gold phase converter, or even the self-referential learning microprocessor.

"No wonder no one from the university ever came by to collect all this stuff," Marla complains. "It's all junk."

Then Marla sees the doorknob. She hadn't noticed it before because it's in a strange place—only a foot or so from the ground, half hidden behind Wilmington's nonfunctioning nuclear refrigerator.

When Ford sees it, his jaw drops with a popping sound. "A tiny door! Do you think Wilmington shrunk himself?"

"Don't be a complete gel-brain," says Marla, brushing her wild hair from her face. "It's just a root cellar. But Wilmington might be in there . . . what's left of him, anyway."

The temptation is too great. Together they push the heavy refrigerator aside, grab the knob, and swing the door wide.

An earthy smell of dry rot wafts out, like the smell of a grave. The door is two feet high, and inside it is pitch black. Together, Marla and Ford step into the root cellar and vanish into darkness.

Through ancient spiderwebs they crawl until they find a dangling string. When they pull it, the room is lit by a single dim bulb that hangs from an earthen ceiling six feet from the ground.

There are no dead bodies down there. The smell is a sack of potatoes that have long since gone to their maker.

But what surrounds them is enough to make their hearts miss several beats.

Razor-sharp gears, knifelike spokes, and huge magnets are frozen in position. The entire room has been converted into one big contraption, and in the center of it is a high-backed chair, its plush upholstery replaced by silver foil.

It looks like the inside of a garbage disposal, thinks Marla.

In the corner sits a pile of dusty notes, and on a control panel is an engraved silver plate that reads:

TEMPUS SYNCRO-EPICYCLUS

"What is it?" wonders Marla. She looks to Ford, whom she has already pegged to be a whiz at this scientific stuff.

Ford swallows a gulp of rotten, stale air. "I think it's a time machine."

It takes a good half hour for them to find the nerve to actually touch the thing. Ford sits on the floor most of that time, reading Wilmington's notes.

"This guy has page after page of physics formulas," Ford tells Marla. "He must have thought he was Einstein or something."

"But does it work?" she asks.

Ford furrows his brow. "I have no idea."

"There's one way to find out," she says, grabbing Ford's sweaty hand.

Together they run upstairs and find the perfect guinea pig; Ford's baby sister's teddy bear, Buffy. They bring Buffy down and set him on the silver chair.

"I don't know," says Ford. "Maybe we ought

to know everything about this machine before we start throwing switches."

"You can't ride a bike unless you get on and pedal," says Marla, "and you can't travel through time unless you throw the switch!"

"But—"

Marla flicks the switch. The gears begin to grind, the electromagnets begin to spin and hum. They duck their heads to keep from being decapitated by the spinning spokes. Static electricity makes Ford's greased hair stand on end like Marla's. The dangling bulb dims.

There is a flash of light, and Buffy the bear is gone, leaving nothing behind but the stinging odor of ozone in the air. The machine grinds itself to a halt.

Ford and Marla are left gasping on the ground.

"In-totally-credible!" screeches Marla. "Now let's bring it back!"

"That's what I was trying to tell you," explains Ford, catching his breath. "According to Wilmington's journal, time travel only works one way. You can go forward in time, but you can never come back."

"That's ridiculous! That's not the way it happens in the movies."

"Maybe time travel doesn't work the way it does in movies," suggests Ford.

But to Marla it doesn't matter at all. The

point is that however time travel works, it *does* work.

Ford looks to see where the dial is set.

"According to this," he says, "we sent the bear three days into the future. If the bear reappears in that chair three days from now, we'll really know if this thing works."

"I hate waiting," says Marla, as she impatiently picks her rhinestoned nails.

Two days later, Marla's parents read her the riot act. That is to say, they sit her down and demand she change her ways, or else.

"Your mother and I are sick and tired of you being so disrespectful," says her father.

"What's to respect?" she growls at them. "Is it my fault I was born into a family of cave-people?"

That makes her parents boil.

"That's it," says her father. "From now on you're going to stop acting like the Queen of Mars, and you're going to start acting like a normal human being. From now on, young lady, no more neon blue lipstick. No more ultra-violet hair. No more radioactive eye shadow. No more automotive parts hanging from your earlobes. N-O-R-M-A-L. Normal! Do you understand me? Or else you get no allowance! Zero! Zilch!"

"You're so backwards!" screams Marla, and she runs to her room and beats up her pillows.

Alone with her thoughts, it doesn't take her long to decide exactly what to do. Without so much as a goodbye, she takes a final look at her room, then climbs out of the window and heads straight to Ford's house.

The sky is clear, filled with a million unblinking stars, and a furious wind howls through the trees. It's a perfect night for time travel.

"Marla," Ford says. "I've been reading Wilmington's notes, and there's something not quite right."

"Don't be an idiot!" Marla shouts in Ford's face. "The machine works—we saw it! We're going and that's final."

"*I'm* not going anywhere," says Ford. "I'm not into future stuff, okay?"

"It figures," huffs Marla. "I'll go by myself, then."

She pulls open the basement door and stomps down the stairs. Ford follows, trying to talk some sense into her.

"There's lots of stuff I'm still trying to figure out," he says.

"Oh yeah?" She whirls and stares impatiently at him. "Like what?"

"Like the name of the machine," Ford says. "It bugs me. *Tempus Syncro-Epicyclus.* I looked up the word *Epicyclus* in the dictionary. It has something to do with Ptolemy."

"Tommy who?" asks Marla.

"Not Tommy, *Ptolemy*. He was an ancient astronomer who believed the Earth was the center of the universe, and the sun revolved around it!"

"So?" she hisses.

"So, he was wrong!" shouts Ford.

Marla shrugs. "What does that have to do with a twentieth-century genius like Wilmington? At this very moment, *he's* probably in the future partying away, and I plan to join him."

Marla impatiently crosses the basement toward the root-cellar door.

"Marla, the last person to touch that machine must have been Wilmington—and it was set for three days! If he went three days into the future, *why didn't he come back?*"

"What are you getting at?"

"I don't know!" says Ford. "I haven't figured it out yet, but I will! Listen, at least wait until tomorrow. If the bear comes back on schedule, you can do whatever you want."

"I can't wait that long. I've got places to go!" shouts Marla.

"You're crazy!" Ford shouts back. "You're the type of person who would dive headfirst into an empty pool, just to find out how empty it is!"

Marla pulls open the root-cellar door, but Ford kicks it closed. The house rattles and moss falls from the peeling walls.

"This is my house, and that means it's my machine," he says. "I won't let you use it, so go home. Now!"

Marla turns her Day-Glo painted eyes to Ford and grits her teeth. "Why you slimy little sluggardly worm-brain! How dare you tell me what I can and cannot do! You think I care what you say, you 'Leave-It-to-Beaver' dweebistic troll? Marla Nixbok does what she wants, *when* she wants to do it, and if you won't throw the switch on that machine, I'll throw it myself!"

Still, Ford refuses to budge, so Marla takes her nails and heartlessly scratches his face, a maneuver she often uses when words no longer work.

Ford grabs his face and yelps in pain. Then he takes his foot away from the door.

"Fine," says Ford. "Go see the future. I hope you materialize right in the middle of a nuclear war!" With that, he storms to the stairs.

Good riddance, thinks Marla. Maybe she ought to travel fifty years into the future, just so she can find Ford as a shriveled old man and laugh in his wrinkled face.

Marla bends down and crawls into the root cellar.

At the top of the basement stairs, the truth finally strikes Buford Planct with such fury that it nearly knocks him down the stairs. If Marla uses that machine, her future won't be nuclear war. It'll be far, far from it.

"No!" he screams, and races back down the stairs.

In the root cellar, Marla turns the knob to "One Year." One year is a good first trip. After that, who knows? Decades! Maybe centuries! At last she'll be free to travel to whatever time and place she feels she belongs. The Queen of Time. She likes the sound of that.

Ford crawls into the root cellar, out of breath.

"Marla, don't!" he screams.

"Get lost!" she shrieks back.

"But I figured it out!"

"Good. Does the machine work?"

"Yes, it does, but—"

"That's all I need to know!" Marla flips the switch and leaps into the silver chair. "See you next year!" she calls.

"Nooooooo!"

But Marla never gets to see the horror in Ford's eyes. Instead she sees a flash of light and is struck by a shock of pain as she is propelled exactly one year into the future, in this, the most exciting moment of her life.

In an instant she understands it all—and it is much worse than diving into an empty pool. Now she knows what Ford had been trying so desperately to tell her, because she is now very, very cold.

And she is floating.

Ford was right: the machine works all too well. She has traveled one year forward in time.

But she isn't the center of the universe.

And neither is the Earth.

Suddenly she remembers that the Earth revolves around the sun, and the sun revolves around the center of the galaxy, and the galaxies are flying apart at millions of miles per hour. Everything in the universe has been moving, except for Marla Nixbok. Marla has appeared in the *exact* location in space that she had been one year ago . . .

But the Earth has long since moved on.

Even the sun is gone—just one among many distant stars.

Now she knows exactly why Wilmington and Buffy the bear can never come back. And as her last breath is sucked out of her lungs by the void of space, Marla Nixbok finally gets what she has always wanted: a crystal-clear vision of her own future. Now, and forever.

This class is a bunch of real cut-ups!

BIOLOGY 205

Jeremy Sabacek

Ring . . . The 7:45 bell rang for Biology 205 lab class. The twenty-one students filed in, chattering among themselves. They talked about the upcoming game, the weekend dance, and after-school activities. They eased into their assigned seats around the three parallel lab tables. As Mr. Neila entered the room, the class focused their attention on him. They were an eager class, and most of them were interested to know what they were going to do in today's lab.

Mr. Neila began the class by giving his usual greeting. He introduced the lab by telling the class that today's work was the dissection of a primitive, simple species that was now very rare. He was enthusiastic as he told them that they were lucky to have three specimens to dissect and observe. He reminded them that as always he was available throughout the entire class to answer any questions or help with any problems that might arise.

Mr. Neila instructed the group leaders to use the scalpel to make an incision along the ventral midline of the specimen. He told the students to be extremely careful in cutting the exterior covering of the specimen, or they might damage the internal organs. After pulling back a portion of the covering, the students were able to observe the interior parts and record their data. Using the forceps, various probes, and scissors, the class gently pulled and stretched the odd-looking organs.

Mr. Neila talked on as the students took turns following his directions on how to remove individual parts and place them carefully into dissecting pans. He said in future classes they would study each of these organs in more detail.

As the lab went on, you could hear various comments as students examined the parts they were removing. "Interesting" . . . "Very odd" . . . "What an inferior digestive system" . . . "Yuck" . . . "Icky" . . . "With this really primitive breathing system it's a wonder they could live . . ."

As class time grew limited, Mr. Neila instructed the group to halt their dissection and finish recording their data.

"Since you only have five minutes left, I just wanted to tell you that you did a very good job on these difficult specimens today. Finish recording your lab observations for tomorrow. There will be a test on this material in two days."

The bell rang. The class rose quickly and proceeded noisily into the hallway. As the last two students passed through the exit, one turned to the other.

"Boy, I sure hope this test is not too difficult," he said as he rubbed an area on his green scaley neck. "My mom said if I don't pass this test on the life processes of *Homo sapiens*, I'm not going to be allowed to go to the dance on Saturn's eighth moon this weekend."

"The test probably will be tricky," the other replied, blinking his three eyes nervously. "Those earthlings are put together in a really weird way."

Probably nothing frightens us more than something—or someone—we just don't understand. . . .

THE MAN UNDER THE BRIDGE

Steve Rasnic Tem

Mike and Charlie were riding their bikes on the path that ran alongside the creek that wound through the center of the city. The path went under highway bridges and under railroad bridges, even under a few buildings.

It had rained all morning, but stopped half an hour earlier. Small, shiny puddles spotted the pavement. A little bit of sun had just slipped around the edge of the clouds. The path took the two boys through deep shadows formed by a wide highway bridge above them. Mike had been looking left and right as they rode scouting for bottles and cans, or anything else they might be able to sell to the recycling place.

"Hey," Charlie said, pointing. "Look at that guy under the bridge."

Mike glanced up from the path and saw a dark form sitting on top of the bank, just under the edge of the bridge. Cardboard boxes were piled around him and wedged into the dark place where the underside of the bridge met the ground.

Mike turned his attention back to the bike path. It got pretty crooked at that point, and he didn't want to end up in the creek. "It's probably just an old homeless guy," he said. "My mom says they start moving under the bridges here late in the fall. When it gets too cold, the police make them go into a shelter. It sounds crazy, but she said a lot of them don't want to go. They'd rather stay under the bridges. I'll never understand people like that."

As Mike steered carefully around the next curve, he discovered that his friend wasn't beside him anymore. Mike put his feet down to stop the bike, then turned around. Charlie was still looking up at the bank.

"Charlie!" Mike called. "Hey, Charlie, let's go!"

Mike turned his bike around and pedaled back. He pulled up alongside Charlie and waited for his friend to say something. But Charlie didn't say a word, didn't even turn his head. It was as if the old man had him hypnotized or something.

"Earth to Charlie. Come in, Charlie."

Nothing.

"Charlie, this is ridiculous! You act like you've never seen a bum before."

That broke Charlie out of his trance. He looked at Mike. "How do you know he's a bum?"

Mike felt a little embarrassed. Maybe "bum" was a rude thing to say. "I didn't mean anything by it. It's just that, well, these old guys have been down here forever. You've seen them before."

"How do you know he's old?" Charlie asked in a soft voice. "I mean, he's pretty far away, and it's kind of dark up there. He could be our age for all you know. In fact, if you squint a little, he kind of looks like Randy."

"Who?"

"You know, that new kid with the speech problem. The one that talks so funny nobody can understand him."

Mike laughed at the idea. "You can't be serious." But he could tell by the look in Charlie's eyes that his friend was serious. "All alone like that? Out in the cold?" Mike looked up at the shadowed figure under the bridge. He couldn't make out any of the features. The underside of the bridge was too dark. Could that really be a teenage boy up there? "You're kidding me, right? Charlie? Did you get a good look at his face?"

"Yeah . . . well, I think I did." Charlie was

staring at the shadowy figure, looking hypnotized again. Mike could hardly stand to watch.

"And you could tell he was a kid our age?"

Charlie turned to Mike. "I didn't say he was for sure, I just asked how you could be so sure he wasn't. I don't know, this is pretty weird. I can't really see who or what it is, but when I look up there, I think I see a man, or a boy, or somebody I used to know, or other times somebody I just haven't met yet."

Mike stared at him. "You're not making much sense. Did you get a good look at his face or not?"

"Sort of. I mean, I think that was his face. But I'm not really sure."

Mike couldn't hide his impatience. "What do you mean, you *think?* A face is a face."

Charlie looked up at the figure again, then jumped back, startled. "But what if it's a roach?"

Mike climbed off his bike and let it fall into the path. "Charlie, are you okay?"

"What if it's a roach?"

"What are you talking about?" Mike exclaimed. "I thought we were talking about that guy up there."

"What if that man's face up there is a roach's face?" Charlie asked Mike.

Mike stood still. He struggled to say something, then stalled, then tried again. "Then I'd say you were dreaming." He paused. "And that

I was in your dream. Or I would say you were crazy. Either way, I think we should get home. Our parents are probably going to kill us for going someplace where you start seeing old men with roach faces."

Charlie didn't say anything. Instead, he climbed off his bike and started up the bank toward the shape under the bridge.

"Charlie!" Mike shouted. But Charlie paid no attention. He kept on climbing. The next thing Mike knew, Charlie was all the way up the bank, face to face with the homeless man.

Mike wanted to leave then, but he couldn't. Charlie was his best friend. So he went up the bank after him, his heart pounding.

When he was only a few feet away, he was surprised to find that he still couldn't quite see the man's face: His head was like a big ball of dough, with bumps and shadows on it. Not really any kind of face at all. And when the guy moved his head, even a little, the bumps and shadows changed, showed up in different places on the big lump of dough that sat on his skinny neck.

And Mike kept hearing this scraping sound, like a piece of wood, or claws, rubbing back and forth against the hard-packed ground. It was like watching a really scary movie. He wanted to close his eyes, but he didn't dare.

"Charlie, this is just too weird," he whispered. "Let's get out of here."

"I don't know what you're talking about. I'm looking at the guy's face, and I don't think it's so bad."

Mike looked over his friend's shoulder. And then, instead of seeing an old homeless man or some monster or shadow, he saw his own grandfather sitting under the bridge. That in itself would be weird enough—his grandfather would never dress in ragged clothes like that—but weirder still was the fact that Mike's grandfather had been dead over a year.

His grandfather's face looked right at Mike and grinned. Mike felt embarrassed: His grandfather had always made him uncomfortable. He'd always seemed so old, and he talked in this funny accent, and most of the time Mike didn't understand half of what he said. Mike was ashamed of himself, but he used to avoid his grandfather whenever the old man visited.

But then the face was a cloudy lump of dough again, not really a face at all.

"Charlie, what do you see now?" Mike whispered. "Do you see what I'm seeing? I mean, the dude has no face."

"Oh, I guess it was too dark," Charlie said. "See, the light's getting a little brighter under here. It's almost sunset, but we can see more. Hey, look—it's not a guy after all. He's a she."

It seemed weird to be talking about this thing, or this person, when it was sitting only a few feet away. But Mike couldn't talk to the thing. It was too much like a movie—this just couldn't be happening. Mike squinted against the light and tried to focus on the face of the figure under the bridge. And sure enough it wasn't an old man's face he was seeing anymore, but the face of a girl. Mike recognized her: Amanda, from his fifth-period math class.

Mike never could speak to Amanda. She wasn't just any girl; she was the most beautiful girl he had ever seen. And the nicest, as far as he could tell, never having spoken to her. She lived in a big house in a part of the city Mike had never visited, and she traveled places Mike had never been and used big words Mike had never heard any other kid their age use. So how could you speak in front of a girl like Amanda? Every time he saw her his tongue seemed to turn into a piece of wood, and the rest of the day he could feel splinters in his lips.

Mike could not imagine what the life of a girl like Amanda must be like.

Then the face was all lumpy clay again. And Mike watched, and stared, as the light changed again, and boiling shadows passed over the face. The face became a dog's face, a lizard's face, a spider's face, a murderer's face, a monster's face, the face of everything he'd ever been afraid of, the face of everything and everyone he could not understand, no matter how hard he tried.

And then the face wasn't a face at all, but a shiny mask that blinked and sparkled in the last rays of the sun as they hit the underside of the bridge. But before it was completely dark, the guy with the alien face stood up and climbed into one of the cardboard boxes wedged far back under the bridge.

The cardboard began to glow, and at first Mike thought it had caught fire. He ran toward the edge of the shallow creek, pulling off his cap, thinking he'd fill it with water to put out the fire.

But when he turned back, the box was floating in the air a few feet above Charlie's head. Mike looked up at Charlie and Charlie looked at Mike. Almost at the same time they raised their hands and waved at the box.

When the box took off and disappeared into the sky, it made a thundering noise that shook the buildings for blocks around.

It was all Mike could talk about at school the next day, when he spoke to Amanda, and the new kid Randy, for the first time.

Michael Markiewicz (pronounced Mar-keh'-vich) has contributed several stories about the young King Arthur to this series of anthologies. Here he tries his hand at something completely different, a story about love and death and hard choices.

ALL IN GOOD TIME

Michael Markiewicz

She was born under a blue moon and had had the "Sight" since she could remember. She often knew things—or saw things—that other people couldn't. But sometimes it didn't help.

The first time Dalia saw the Boneman, she was six. He was walking through her grand-mother's rose garden. She stopped him, staring at his coal-black suit and the hourglass in his right hand, and glanced at the house behind her. She knew what was happening in the up-stairs room. She knew why the family had driven up the mountain, past the mines and smelting factories, to the little house that al-ways smelled like flowers.

"Are you going inside?" she had asked.

The Boneman nodded.

" 'Cause my Gram's dying?"

He looked sad and happy at the same time, but he didn't answer. He went to push past her, but Dalia moved her tiny body into his path.

"I'm here for your grandmother, sweetie," he said with a gentle breeze for a voice. His breath was calm and cool and soft.

"You're going to take her away?"

The figure nodded again.

"I'm the . . . Boneman," he replied, though it seemed as if that wasn't his real name.

"And you take people?"

"All in good time."

He swirled past her like a dark cloud of soot from one of the smokestacks. Before she could do anything, Death walked into the house . . . and her grandmother was gone.

Her grandfather moved in with Dalia and her mother after that. Her father had left when she was just a baby, and it was nice to have Paps around the house. At first it was a little strange, but then she discovered that she and Paps had something special. They both loved to fish in the pond out back, and they would spend hours casting and talking. She could tell him about things she saw, and he took her seriously.

Perhaps it was the Sight, but she felt more

at home with older people. Paps understood her better than kids her age did, and sometimes, she could tell him about the things she saw.

But it was five years later, and Dalia knew the Boneman would come again, in good time.

"I've brought my Seder plate," announced Dalia's aunt Eunice as she and Uncle Roger strolled into the house. Eunice was always the happy younger sister of the family, but she radiated even more lately. Even with Paps so sick she still managed a silly grin as she set the table with the china.

"I don't know if he'll make it down," said Carolyn, Dalia's mother. Her forehead was creased with the worry line she always got when things weren't right.

But Dalia knew he would make it, and she knew that she would have to ask the questions again.

Every year the same questions, and it all seemed quite stupid to her.

"Why do we eat matzah?"

"Why is this night different?"

Why is the sky blue? she thought sarcastically.

All the adults would compliment her, pinch her cheeks, and tell her what a good girl she was. She hated every minute of it.

"I'll help Paps," said Dalia while her aunt and mom got out the Haggadah prayer books

and prepared for the Passover service. They didn't follow the laws, but Passover was still special for the family. Her aunt Gwen had brought a leg of lamb for dinner and said it wasn't proper, but then nothing these days was proper.

Paps was coughing when she came into his room.

"They're ready," she said as the old man pulled himself to the bed's edge.

"Okay, Dalia," he whispered roughly. "You know, I may not see another Seder with the shape I'm in."

Dalia knew that before he said it. She'd heard the doctor talking to her mother the week before.

"You'll be fine," she insisted.

The old man paused and looked out the window at the pond just past their small yard. A fish jumped, sending out ripples near their favorite spot.

"You may have to bait your own hooks this summer," he said somberly.

Dalia shook her head.

"You know I can't do it," she argued. "It makes me sick. So you'll just *have* to be here to help me."

"Dalia, you know I'm not well."

She nodded.

"I was talking to your grandmother, and she thinks it's just about my time."

Dalia's eyes widened.

"But she's dead, Paps."

The old man smiled.

"Oh, she's not that far, really. You have the Sight. You ought to know that we're never really far from people we love. But I think she and I will be closer soon."

"You're not going anywhere, Paps!" she yelled.

He swallowed.

"I know it's hard, Dal, but there's a time for everything. I've missed your grandmother so bad these five years. I guess I'll be glad to be with her again. All my old friends are gone. . . . It's just my time."

Dalia wanted to cry, but she pushed it back.

Paps hugged her tenderly.

"I'll never be that far from you," he whispered, and she knew it was a promise. But it wasn't what she wanted.

Dalia helped him to his feet, and he coughed again. They walked down the split-level stairs slowly, as though descending a huge tower, and came to the dining room arm in arm.

"Hi, Dad," said Aunt Eunice. "I've got some good news."

Paps smiled. He seemed to know before she told him, but it was still wonderful. She and

Roger were expecting a baby. Paps was going to be a grandfather again, and his chest seemed to be strong for just a few minutes.

The old man took his seat at the head of the table and leaned heavily on a pillow to his left. They retold the Bible story like they did every year: the tale of Moses leading the Israelites out of slavery in Egypt, of those terrible plagues that God used to convince the Egyptians to let his people go. And Dalia asked the questions even though she hated it. Mostly, she did it for Paps.

"Why do we eat matzah?"

"To remind us of the bread our ancestors ate."

"Why bitter herbs?"

"To remind us of the bitterness of slavery."

Then they read through the part about the lamb's blood on the door lintel. It explained how the blood was a sign so that the Angel of Death would not come into the Israelites' houses. Instead, he would kill only the firstborn of the Egyptians.

"When I see the blood I will pass over you . . . and I will not let the destroyer enter your houses."

Dalia listened to the familiar words as she recited them with Paps. He coughed as they read and held his chest tightly. And then, possibly for the first time, she heard the story, really heard it. Something clicked . . . and she understood.

As her grandfather began one of the prayers, his coughing got worse. But during that prayer Dalia quietly smiled and smelled the dinner cooking in the kitchen.

They read aloud the last portion of the service, and Paps began to choke uncontrollably. He covered his mouth and tried to be polite, but it was impossible. That night, after the Seder was over and the house was dark, Dalia knew what she had to do.

She waited until her mother and Paps were asleep. Then she went to the refrigerator and took out a leftover tidbit of lamb with just the smallest trace of blood. There wasn't much, but the story didn't say you needed a lot. Maybe just a few drops would be enough.

Dalia took the stepladder from behind the refrigerator and carried it to the front porch. She stood in the open doorway and smeared the meat over the door's lintel, making sure it left just a faint streak. No one but her, and the Boneman, would know.

Paps still coughed. In the following days he spit up blood several times, but Dalia had faith. If he didn't get better, at least she knew he wouldn't die. The Boneman wouldn't get in this time.

*   *   *

It was nearly two o'clock in the morning when she heard the knock on the front door. It was a loud, hollow pounding that woke her. The door beat again, triplets that echoed in the split-level stairwell like a huge hammer.

Her mother and Paps seemed unaware of the late visitor, but the pounding got more and more intense until Dalia had to do something. It seemed to shake the walls of her room and the insides of her head. Finally she made her way downstairs to the foyer.

She peered cautiously through the spy glass in the front door. In the faint streetlight stood a tall figure in a neat black suit. His right hand held a large hourglass.

He was not a burglar.

"What do you want?" asked the girl through the door.

"I'm afraid it's time," he replied.

"Time?" she asked sharply. "Time for what? It's two in the morning."

"I'm sorry, but it is time for your grandfather to accompany me." The man seemed concerned, and straightforward about his duty. "I wouldn't have disturbed you," he continued, "but I'm not able to come in without your help. You see, there is a problem with your door."

"I did it," she explained.

"You did it?"

"I put the blood on the door so you wouldn't take Paps."

"You know who I am and why I am here, Dalia?"

The girl looked down at the carpet. She wasn't sure if it was the right thing to do, but she was not going to lose Paps, no matter what.

"Are you the . . . Angel of Death?"

"Yes," answered the stranger through the steel-core door that seemed to bend under his breath.

"If you don't let me in I will have to take someone else in his place."

"Fine," she spit.

"Surely, you can see that this is not wise."

The girl thought.

"Will you let me in?"

"No."

"Dalia," said Death, "I must leave soon."

"I don't care!" she cried. "I'll never let you in!"

Her eyes glazed. She was afraid and confused.

"Dalia—"

"Go away!" she screamed and ran into the living room. The angel knocked three more times and then was gone.

The sound of sirens woke everyone at six that morning. A car had skittered off the road and struck a tree just down the street. The neighbors said it was drunk driving, but Dalia thought it was something else. As the ambulance pulled away she wondered if the driver would survive. She wondered if he was to take Paps' place. She thought about the terrible power that she was playing with. And, despite her hopes, she felt sick with guilt.

That night Dalia couldn't sleep. She tossed and turned for hours and listened to the snoring and occasional hacks from her grandfather in the next room. One moment she would feel as though she were a murderer, and then the next she would think of losing her best, her only real, friend. She was convinced that the man in the accident had paid for Paps. It had to be. It just had to be. But three minutes before two A.M. the front door felt a hard bony fist again.

The house shook, but her mother and Paps slept undisturbed.

Only Dalia was awakened by the horrible beating. She was more than frightened, but she wasn't ready to change her mind. The angel still hadn't taken someone for Paps. The accident must have been just that. But her grandfather would not die. Not tonight. Not tomorrow. Not ever.

After what seemed like an eternity the pounding stopped and the angel went elsewhere.

*   *   *

"Oh, no!" Carolyn cried as she clutched the kitchen telephone tighter. "She's . . . Oh, my . . . All right, all right . . . Yes, we'll be there. . . . I'll see if he can come."

Dalia sat at the breakfast table, her eyes opening wider and wider. Fear crept up her neck and across her face as her mother put down the receiver.

And Dalia knew what her mother was about to say before she spoke.

"It's your aunt Eunice," said Carolyn. "She had an accident. She fell down the steps in her house."

"Is she . . . dead?" Dalia asked with a crack in her voice.

"She's in critical condition."

Suddenly Paps was at the head of the stairs looking into the kitchen.

"And the baby?" he asked, leaning heavily on the railing.

Carolyn paused.

"They don't know if it will make it."

Dalia swallowed hard. She felt a knot building in her throat, and something made her stomach boil. A stranger, maybe, but her aunt Eunice? Or the baby? Dalia could barely control the quiver in her jaw or the panic in her eyes.

"Let's go to the hospital," said Paps as he

struggled down the steps and plucked his sweater from the sofa.

"Are you going to be all right?" asked Carolyn, but Dalia knew he wouldn't be. He couldn't leave. He couldn't go outside the protection of the blood-stained door.

Paps moved toward the foyer as Dalia's heart raced faster and faster. She had to stop him. She had to.

"Paps, you can't go!" she screamed.

"I have to go, Dal."

"But you can't! Please, let me explain."

Dalia pulled him into the kitchen while her mother waited, bewildered, by the front door. Carolyn didn't understand the Sight, but Paps would.

Dalia explained the whole thing—how she had seen the angel and how the blood had worked . . . and how someone had to die in his place.

Paps' face faded to white as Dalia told him. He held his chest and pushed back his hair. He took a long breath, and then turned to the door.

"Paps?" she asked in a confused whisper. "You're going anyway?"

"I'm afraid so, Dalia," he answered. "But it's all right. There's a time for all things. Even a time for dying."

"I don't want you to die, Paps!" she cried.

He held her tightly, tighter than his weak arms were really capable of.

"It's not fair. It's just not fair," she sobbed as tears ran down her cheeks and fell on her toes.

The old man looked at her carefully.

"Dalia," he said sternly, "Eunice is my daughter. You have the Sight, you know it's my time. Fair has little to do with it."

They moved through the door together, Dalia clutching Paps' arm like a vise. As they got closer to the car, she could hear the panic in her own heart as it thumped erratically against her ribs. She knew *he* was there. Death was waiting in the bushes or under the Oldsmobile. She scanned the shadows, looking for his dark suit and the cold, impersonal hourglass.

Her mother unlocked the car doors, and Dalia noticed a sudden chill in the air. It was an unmistakable feeling that she recognized as his awful presence, but the angel didn't appear. He seemed to be waiting for something.

She had expected the Boneman to suddenly leap upon them, but, for some reason, it wasn't the right time. Dalia wondered if he had already taken the baby or Eunice—or both. It seemed to her that Death could be cruel enough to take an extra life, just for spite.

Her mother raced them to the hospital, pushing the old sedan through the heavy morning traffic, while Dalia held her breath at every turn of the wheel. They helped Paps inside and quickly found the room where Eunice lay unconscious.

She was lying in a bed with tubes and wires attached to her. Her face was gray and there was a pronounced bruise on the edge of her forehead. Roger was sitting by her side, his eyes dark with worry.

Dalia didn't see the Boneman there, but she felt as though she were being watched.

"Did I do this?" she wondered aloud.

Her uncle looked at her strangely.

"Dalia," Roger answered, "don't be ridiculous. Eunice has been bugging me to fix the carpet on those steps for days. If it's anyone's fault, it's mine."

"Not if she dies," Dalia whispered to herself.

There was a faint breeze from the window, and suddenly she knew what the Boneman was doing. He was giving her a choice. A clear, cold, horrible choice.

"Oh, Eunice," sobbed Paps. "You're so young. . . ."

And he looked at Dalia with large tear-filled eyes.

Dalia could see in his troubled stare what he wanted. The Sight made it easy for her to understand. She looked back, thinking harder than she had ever thought before. She looked and cried and finally turned to the window for relief.

The monitors seemed to give no clue to Eunice's condition, and when Gwen arrived, an hour later, there was still no news. The nurses went in and out, but no one could predict the future. No one but Dalia, who stood weeping by the window.

After long hours of waiting, they were told to go home. The doctor assured them that the hospital would call if there was any change.

They drove away in silence with only an occasional whimper or nervous sniffle. Paps looked at her once, just before they pulled in front of the house, and Dalia again saw the pain in his eyes. Anyone could see it, but she could see deeper than most people. Sometimes the Sight was a terrible thing.

As she stepped through her front door, Dalia looked up and saw the pale streak of blood.

"I'll be right back," she whispered as they entered the dark foyer.

She went to the kitchen and returned with the stepladder and a small rag.

Her mother was busy calling the rest of the family, so she didn't see. But Paps watched as Dalia wiped off the top of the door lintel . . . and there was a cool breeze suddenly blowing through the house.

Her grandfather smiled.

"Thank you, Dalia," he said softly.

It was two A.M., two nights later, when Dalia awoke and stared at the door to her room. The air had turned cold. There was an intruder in the house. But it wasn't a stranger. It was *him*. Death passed by her door as she pushed herself out of bed and into the hall behind him.

"I guess it's time," she said, holding back a tear.

The man in the dark suit stopped. He turned toward her and looked at the hourglass in his hand.

"It's well past time," he said, his breath softly blowing back her hair.

She wondered why he hadn't come sooner. That first night she had hardly slept, expecting Paps to be taken at any moment.

"I thought you deserved some time," the spirit answered, as though he heard her unspoken question. "You're a very brave girl, and you did the right thing in the end."

Dalia could see that the sand had run out, and she quivered as he held the glass in front of him. She wanted to cry or scream or do something, but there was nothing to do.

Then, behind the phantom, there was another shadow. It was her grandfather.

He walked slowly toward them and stood beside the Boneman.

"Do my old friends miss me?" Paps asked with a slight grin.

Death looked at him and smiled.

"They see you every day," the Boneman answered. "But I think they'll be happy now that you're here."

"Here?" asked Dalia.

"I told you, Dal," said the old man. "You have the Sight. I'll never be that far, especially from you."

He hugged her and it was so strong and tight that she could hardly breathe. But when he let go, she could tell that it was not a material arm that had surrounded her.

She stepped to the door of his room and saw Paps lying still in his bed.

"It's okay," whispered her grandfather from behind her. He took hold of Death's sleeve and walked down the hall. "I promised I'll be around from time to time . . . and I always keep my promises."

"All in good time," added the Boneman.

And they faded into the darkness.

As the sun lit her bedroom window hours later, Dalia heard the phone ring and she knew it was the hospital. She also knew Eunice and the baby were going to be all right. And Paps was gone.

She went downstairs without stopping at her grandfather's door. For a moment, she stared at the sweater he had left lying on the sofa. Then, slowly, she walked to the kitchen window and looked toward the pond.

There was a familiar figure standing straight and strong in the shadows near their favorite fishing hole. She could see him clearly, and the faint silhouette of her grandmother by his side. They both looked happy, and Paps waved to her before disappearing in the bright morning sun. And Dalia knew that he wasn't really that far.

I have always felt that forests are the likeliest
places to find magic. A proper forest is deep,
mysterious, strange—and scary. . . .

THE TOADSTOOL WOOD

James Reeves

The toadstool wood is dark and mouldy,
    And has a ferny smell.
About the trees hangs something quiet
    And queer—like a spell.

Beneath the arching sprays of bramble
    Small creatures make their holes;
Over the moss's close green velvet
    The stilted spider strolls.

The stalks of toadstools pale and slender
    That grow from that old log,
Bars they might be to imprison
    A prince turned to a frog.

There lives no mumbling witch nor wizard
    In this uncanny place,
Yet you might think you saw at twilight
    A little, crafty face.

I first read this story more than twenty years ago. Unlike many stories I read that far back, I have never forgotten it. Partly, I suppose, because I always wanted to grow giant mushrooms in my cellar myself. And partly because in its own quiet way it is quite deliciously terrifying.

COME INTO MY CELLAR

Ray Bradbury

Hugh Fortnum woke to Saturday's commotions, and lay, eyes shut, savoring each in its turn.

Below, bacon in a skillet; Cynthia waking him with fine cookings instead of cries.

Across the hall, Tom *actually* taking a shower.

Far off in the bumble-bee dragon-fly light, whose voice was already cursing the weather, the time, and the tides? Mrs. Goodbody? Yes. That Christian giantess, six feet tall with her shoes off, the gardener extraordinary, the octogenarian-dietitian and town philosopher.

He rose, unhooked the screen, and leaned out to hear her cry:

"There! Take *that! This'll* fix you! Hah!"

"Happy Saturday, Mrs. Goodbody!"

The old woman froze in clouds of bug spray pumped from an immense gun.

"Nonsense!" she shouted. "With these fiends and pests to watch for?"

"What kind *this* time?" called Fortnum.

"I don't want to shout it to the jaybirds, but—" she glanced suspiciously around—"what would you say if I told you I was the first line of defense concerning Flying Saucers?"

"Fine," replied Fortnum. "There'll be rockets between the worlds any year now."

"There already *are!*" She pumped, aiming the spray under the hedge. "There! Take that!"

He pulled his head back in from the fresh day, somehow not as high-spirited as his first response had indicated. Poor soul, Mrs. Goodbody. Always the very essence of reason. And now what? Old age?

The doorbell rang.

He grabbed his robe and was half down the stairs when he heard a voice say, "Special Delivery. Fortnum?" and saw Cynthia turn from the front door, a small packet in her hand.

He put his hand out, but she shook her head. "Special Delivery Air Mail for your son."

Tom was downstairs like a centipede.

"Wow! That must be from the Great Bayou Novelty Greenhouse!"

"I wish I were as excited about ordinary mail," observed Fortnum.

"Ordinary?!" Tom ripped the cord and paper wildly. "Don't you read the back pages of *Popular Mechanics?* Well, here *they* are!"

Everyone peered into the small open box.

"Here," said Fortnum, "*what* are?"

"The Sylvan Glade Jumbo-Giant Guaranteed Growth Raise-Them-in-Your-Cellar-for-Big-Profit Mushrooms!"

"Oh, of course," said Fortnum. "How silly of me."

Cynthia squinted. "Those little teeny bits—?"

" 'Fabulous growth in twenty-four hours,' " Tom quoted from memory. " 'Plant them in your own cellar—' "

Fortnum and wife exchanged glances.

"Well," she admitted, "it's better than frogs and green snakes."

"Sure is!" Tom ran.

"Oh, Tom," said Fortnum, lightly.

Tom paused at the cellar door.

"Tom," said his father. "Next time, fourth-class mail would do fine."

"Heck," said Tom. "They must've made a mistake, thought I was some rich company. Air mail special, who can afford *that?*"

The cellar door slammed.

Fortnum, bemused, scanned the wrapper a moment, then dropped it into the wastebasket. On his way to the kitchen, he opened the cellar door.

Tom was already on his knees, digging with a handrake in the dirt of the back part of the cellar.

He felt his wife beside him, breathing softly, looking down into the cool dimness.

"Those *are* mushrooms, I hope. Not . . . toadstools?"

Fortnum laughed. "Happy harvest, farmer!"

Tom glanced up and waved.

Fortnum shut the door, took his wife's arm, and walked her out to the kitchen, feeling fine.

Toward noon, Fortnum was driving toward the nearest market when he saw Roger Willis, a fellow Rotarian, and teacher of biology at the town high school, waving urgently from the sidewalk.

Fortnum pulled his car up and opened the door.

"Hi, Roger, give you a lift?"

Willis responded all too eagerly, jumping in and slamming the door.

"Just the man I want to see. I've put off calling for days. Could you play psychiatrist for five minutes, God help you?"

Fortnum examined his friend for a moment as he drove quietly on.

"God help you, yes. Shoot."

Willis sat back and studied his fingernails. "Let's just drive a moment. There. Okay. Here's what I want to say: something's wrong with the world."

Fortnum laughed easily. "Hasn't there always been?"

"No, no, I mean . . . something strange— something unseen—is happening."

"Mrs. Goodbody," said Fortnum, half to himself, and stopped.

"Mrs. Goodbody?"

"This morning. Gave me a talk on flying saucers."

"No." Willis bit the knuckle of his forefinger nervously. "Nothing like saucers. At least I don't think. Tell me, what is intuition?"

"The conscious recognition of something that's been subconscious for a long time. But don't quote this amateur psychologist!" He laughed again.

"Good, good!" Willis turned, his face lighting. He readjusted himself in the seat. "That's it! Over a long period, things gather, right? All of a sudden, you have to spit, but you don't remember saliva collecting. Your hands are dirty, but you don't know how they got that way. Dust falls on you every day and you don't

105

feel it. But when you get enough dust collected up, there it is, you see and name it. That's intuition, as far as I'm concerned. Well, what kind of dust has been falling on *me?* A few meteors in the sky at night? Funny weather just before dawn? I don't know. Certain colors, smells, the way the house creaks at three in the morning? Hair prickling on my arms? All I know is, the dust *has* collected. Quite suddenly I *know."*

"Yes," said Fortnum, disquieted. "But what *is* it you know?"

Willis looked at his hands in his lap.

"I'm afraid. I'm not afraid. Then I'm afraid again, in the middle of the day. Doctor's checked me. I'm A-1. No family problems. Joe's a fine boy, a good son. Dorothy? She's remarkable. With her, I'm not afraid of growing old or dying."

"Lucky man."

"But beyond my luck now. Scared stiff, really, for myself, my family; even, right now, for *you.*"

"Me?" said Fortnum.

They had stopped now by an empty lot near the market. There was a moment of great stillness, in which Fortnum turned to survey his friend. Willis's voice had suddenly made him cold.

"I'm afraid for everybody," said Willis. "Your

friends, mine, and their friends, on out of sight. Pretty silly, eh?"

Willis opened the door, got out, and peered in at Fortnum. Fortnum felt he had to speak.

"Well—what do we *do* about it?"

Willis looked up at the sun burning blind in the great, remote sky.

"Be aware," he said, slowly. "Watch everything for a few days."

"Everything?"

"We don't use half what God gave us, ten per cent of the time. We ought to hear more, feel more, smell more, taste more. Maybe there's something wrong with the way the wind blows these weeds there in the lot. Maybe it's the sun up on those telephone wires or the cicadas singing in the elm trees. If only we could stop, look, listen, a few days, a few nights, and compare notes. Tell me to shut up then, and I will."

"Good enough," said Fortnum, playing it lighter than he felt. "I'll look around. But how do I know the thing I'm looking for when I *see* it?"

Willis peered in at him sincerely. "You'll know. You've got to know. Or we're done for, all of us," he said quietly.

Fortnum shut the door, and didn't know what to say. He felt a flush of embarrassment creeping up his face. Willis sensed this.

"Hugh, do you think I'm—off my rocker?"

"Nonsense!" said Fortnum, too quickly. "You're just nervous, is all. You should take a couple of weeks off."

Willis nodded. "See you Monday night?"

"Any time. Drop around."

"I hope I will, Hugh. I really hope I will."

Then Willis was gone, hurrying across the dry weed-grown lot, toward the side entrance of the market.

Watching him go, Fortnum suddenly did not want to move. He discovered that very slowly he was taking deep breaths, weighing the silence. He licked his lips, tasting the salt. He looked at his arm on the doorsill, the sunlight burning the golden hairs. In the empty lot the wind moved all alone to itself. He leaned out to look at the sun, which stared back with one massive stunning blow of intense power that made him jerk his head in.

He exhaled. Then he laughed out loud. Then he drove away.

The lemonade glass was cool and deliciously sweaty. The ice made music inside the glass, and the lemonade was just sour enough, just sweet enough on his tongue. He sipped, he savored, he tilted back in the wicker rocking chair on the twilight front porch, his eyes closed. The crickets were chirping out on the lawn. Cynthia, knitting across from him on the porch, eyed him curiously. He could feel the pressure of her attention.

"What are you up to?" she said at last.

"Cynthia," he said, "is your intuition in running order? Is this earthquake weather? Is the land going to sink? Will war be declared? Or is it only that our delphinium will die of the blight?"

"Hold on. Let me feel my bones."

He opened his eyes and watched Cynthia in turn closing hers and sitting absolutely statue-still, her hands on her knees. Finally she shook her head and smiled.

"No. No war declared. No land sinking. Not even a blight. Why?"

"I've met a lot of Doom Talkers today. Well, two, anyway, and—"

The screen door burst wide. Fortnum's body jerked as if he had been struck. "What!"

Tom, a gardener's wooden flat in his arms, stepped out on the porch.

"Sorry," he said. "What's wrong, Dad?"

"Nothing," Fortnum stood up, glad to be moving. "Is that the crop?"

Tom moved forward, eagerly. "Part of it. Boy, they're doing great. In just seven hours, with lots of water, look how big the darn things are!" He set the flat on the table between his parents.

The crop was indeed plentiful. Hundreds of

small grayish brown mushrooms were sprouting up in the damp soil.

"I'll be. . . ." said Fortnum, impressed.

Cynthia put out her hand to touch the flat, then took it away uneasily.

"I hate to be a spoilsport, but . . . there's no way for these to be anything else but mushrooms, is there?"

Tom looked as if he had been insulted. "What do you think I'm going to feed you? Poison fungoids?"

"That's just it," said Cynthia quickly. "How do you tell them apart?"

"Eat 'em," said Tom. "If you live, they're mushrooms. If you drop dead—*well!*"

He gave a great guffaw, which amused Fortnum, but only made his mother wince. She sat back in her chair.

"I—I don't like them," she said.

"Boy, oh, boy." Tom seized the flat angrily. "When are we going to have the next Wet Blanket Sale in *this* house!?"

He shuffled morosely away.

"Tom—" said Fortnum.

"Never mind," said Tom. "Everyone figures they'll be ruined by the boy entrepreneur. To heck with it!"

Fortnum got inside just as Tom heaved the mushrooms, flat and all, down the cellar stairs.

He slammed the cellar door and ran angrily out the back door.

Fortnum turned back to his wife, who, stricken, glanced away.

"I'm sorry," she said. "I don't know why, I just *had* to say that to Tom."

The phone rang. Fortnum brought the phone outside on its extension cord.

"Hugh?" It was Dorothy Willis's voice. She sounded suddenly very old and very frightened. "Hugh . . . Roger isn't there, is he?"

"Dorothy? No."

"He's gone!" said Dorothy. "All his clothes were taken from the closet." She began to cry softly.

"Dorothy, hold on, I'll be there in a minute."

"You must help, oh, you must. Something's happened to him, I know it," she wailed. "Unless you do something, we'll never see him alive again."

Very slowly, he put the receiver back on its hook, her voice weeping inside it. The night crickets, quite suddenly, were very loud. He felt the hairs, one by one, go up on the back of his neck.

Hair can't do that, he thought. Silly, silly. It can't do that, not in *real* life, it can't!

But, one by slow pricking one, his hair did.

The wire hangers were indeed empty. With a clatter, Fortnum shoved them aside and down along the rod, then turned and looked out of the closet at Dorothy Willis and her son, Joe.

"I was just walking by," said Joe, "and saw the closet empty, all Dad's clothes gone!"

"Everything was fine," said Dorothy. "We've had a wonderful life. I don't understand it, I don't, I don't!" She began to cry again, putting her hands to her face.

Fortnum stepped out of the closet.

"You didn't hear him leave the house?"

"We were playing catch out front," said Joe. "Dad said he had to go in for a minute. I went around back. Then—he was gone!"

"He must have packed quickly and walked wherever he was going, so we wouldn't hear a cab pull up front of the house."

They were moving out through the hall now.

"I'll check the train depot and the airport." Fortnum hesitated. "Dorothy, is there anything in Roger's background—"

"It wasn't insanity took him." She hesitated. "I feel—somehow—he was kidnapped."

Fortnum shook his head. "It doesn't seem reasonable he would arrange to pack, walk out of the house, and go meet his abductors."

Dorothy opened the door as if to let the night or the night wind move down the hall as she turned to stare back through the rooms, her voice wandering.

"No. Somehow they came into the house. Right in front of us, they stole him away."

And then:

". . . a terrible thing has happened."

Fortnum stepped out into the night of crickets and rustling trees. The Doom Talkers, he thought, talking their Dooms. Mrs. Goodbody. Roger. And now Roger's wife. Something terrible *has* happened. But *what*, in God's name? And *how?*

He looked from Dorothy to her son. Joe, blinking the wetness from his eyes, took a long time to turn, walk along the hall, and stop, fingering the knob of the cellar door.

Fortnum felt his eyelids twitch, his iris flex, as if he were snapping a picture of something he wanted to remember.

Joe pulled the cellar door wide, stepped down out of sight, gone. The door tapped shut.

Fortnum opened his mouth to speak, but Dorothy's hand was taking his now, he had to look at her.

"Please," she said. "Find him for me."

He kissed her cheek. "If it's humanly possible . . ."

If it's humanly possible. Good Lord, why had he picked those words?

He walked off into the summer night.

*   *   *

A gasp, an exhalation, a gasp, an exhalation, an asthmatic insuck, a vaporing sneeze. Someone dying in the dark? No.

Just Mrs. Goodbody, unseen beyond the hedge, working late, her hand pump aimed, her bony elbow thrusting. The sick-sweet smell of bug spray enveloped Fortnum heavily as he reached his house.

"Mrs. Goodbody? Still at it?!"

From the black hedge, her voice leapt:

"Blast it, yes! Aphids, waterbugs, woodworms, and now the *marasmius oreades*. Lord, it grows fast!"

"What does?"

"The *marasmius oreades*, of course! It's me against them, and I intend to win. There! There! There!"

He left the hedge, the gasping pump, the wheezing voice, and found his wife waiting for him on the porch almost as if she were going to take up where Dorothy had left off at her door a few minutes ago.

Fortnum was about to speak, when a shadow moved inside. There was a creaking noise. A knob rattled.

Tom vanished into the basement.

Fortnum felt as if someone had set off an explosion in his face. He reeled. Everything had the numbed familiarity of those waking dreams where all motions are remembered before they occur, all dialogue known before it fell from the lips.

He found himself staring at the shut basement door. Cynthia took him inside, amused.

"What? Tom? Oh, I relented. The darn mushrooms meant so much to him. Besides, when he threw them into the cellar, they did nicely, just lying in the dirt."

"Did they?" Fortnum heard himself say.

Cynthia took his arm. "What about Roger?"

"He's gone, yes."

"Men, men, men," she said.

"No, you're wrong," he said. "I saw Roger every day for the last ten years. When you know a man that well, you can tell how things are at home, whether things are in the oven or the mixmaster. Death hadn't breathed down his neck yet. He wasn't running scared after his immortal youth, picking peaches in someone else's orchards. No, no, I swear, I'd bet my last dollar on it, Roger—"

The doorbell rang behind him. The delivery boy had come up quietly onto the porch and was standing there with a telegram in his hand.

"Fortnum?"

Cynthia snapped on the hall light as he ripped the envelope open and smoothed it out for reading.

"TRAVELING NEW ORLEANS. THIS TELEGRAM POSSIBLE OFF-GUARD MOMENT. YOU MUST

REFUSE, REPEAT REFUSE, ALL SPECIAL DELIVERY
PACKAGES! ROGER."

Cynthia glanced up from the paper.
"I don't understand. What does he mean?"
But Fortnum was already at the telephone,
dialing swiftly, once. "Operator? The police,
and hurry!"

At ten-fifteen that night, the phone rang for the
sixth time during the evening. Fortnum got it, and
immediately gasped. "Roger! Where are you?"
"Where am I?" said Roger lightly, almost
amused. "You know very well where I am.
You're responsible for this. I should be
angry!"
Cynthia, at his nod, had hurried to take the
extension phone in the kitchen. When he heard
the soft click, he went on.
"Roger, I swear I don't know. I got that telegram from you—"
"What telegram?" said Roger, jovially. "I
sent no telegram. Now, of a sudden, the police
come pouring onto the southbound train, pull
me off in some jerkwater, and I'm calling you
to get them off my neck. Hugh, if this is some
joke—"
"But, Roger, you just vanished!"
"On a business trip. If you can call that van-
ishing. I told Dorothy about this, and Joe."

"This is all very confusing, Roger. You're in no danger? Nobody's blackmailing you, forcing you into this speech?"

"I'm fine, healthy, free, and unafraid."

"But, Roger, your premonitions . . . ?"

"Poppycock! Now, look, I'm being very good about this, aren't I?"

"Sure, Roger."

"Then play the good father and give me permission to go. Call Dorothy and tell her I'll be back in five days. How *could* she have forgotten?"

"She did, Roger. See you in five days, then?"

"Five days, I swear."

The voice was indeed winning and warm, the old Roger again. Fortnum shook his head, more bewildered than before.

"Roger," he said, "this is the craziest day I've ever spent. You're not running off from Dorothy? Good Lord, you can tell *me.*"

"I love her with all my heart. Now, here's Lieutenant Parker of the Ridgetown police. Goodbye, Hugh."

"Good—"

But the lieutenant was on the line, talking angrily. What had Fortnum meant putting them to this trouble? What was going on? Who did he think he was? Did or didn't he want this so-called friend held or released?

"Released," Fortnum managed to say somewhere along the way, and hung up the phone and imagined he heard a voice call all aboard and the massive thunder of the train leaving the station two hundred miles south in the somehow increasingly dark night.

Cynthia walked very slowly into the parlor.

"I feel so foolish," she said.

"How do you think I feel?"

"Who could have sent that telegram? And why?"

He poured himself some Scotch and stood in the middle of the room looking at it.

"I'm glad Roger is all right," his wife said, at last.

"He isn't," said Fortnum.

"But you just said—"

"I said nothing. After all, we couldn't very well drag him off that train and truss him up and send him home, could we, if he insisted he was okay? No. He sent that telegram, but he changed his mind after sending it. Why, why, why?" Fortnum paced the room, sipping the drink. "Why warn us against special delivery packages? The only package we've got this *year* which fits that description is the one Tom got this morning—" His voice trailed off.

Before he could move, Cynthia was at the wastepaper basket taking out the crumpled wrapping paper with the special-delivery stamps on it.

The postmark read: New Orleans, LA.

Cynthia looked up from it. "New Orleans. Isn't that where Roger is heading right *now?*"

A doorknob rattled, a door opened and closed in Fortnum's mind. Another doorknob rattled, another door swung wide and then shut. There was a smell of damp earth.

He found his hand dialing the phone. After a long while, Dorothy Willis answered at the other end. He could imagine her sitting alone in a house with too many lights on. He talked quietly with her awhile, then cleared his throat and said, "Dorothy, look. I know it sounds silly. Did any special delivery air mail packages arrive at your house the last few days?"

Her voice was faint. "No." Then: "No, wait. Three days ago. But I thought you *knew!* All the boys on the block are going in for it."

Fortnum measured his words carefully.

"Going in for what?"

"But why ask?" she said. "There's nothing wrong with raising mushrooms, is there?"

Fortnum closed his eyes.

"Hugh? Are you still there?" asked Dorothy. "I said: there's nothing wrong with—"

"—raising mushrooms?" said Fortnum, at last. "No. Nothing wrong. Nothing wrong."

And slowly he put down the phone.

The curtains blew like veils of moonlight. The clock ticked. The after-midnight world flowed into and filled the bedroom. He heard Mrs. Goodbody's clear voice on this morning's air, a million years gone now. He heard Roger putting a cloud over the sun at noon. He heard the police cursing him by phone from downstate. Then Roger's voice again, with the locomotive thunder hurrying him away and away, fading. And finally, Mrs. Goodbody's voice behind the hedge:

"Lord, it grows fast!"

"What does?"

"Marasmius oreades!"

He snapped his eyes open. He sat up.

Downstairs, a moment later, he flicked through the unabridged dictionary.

His forefinger underlined the words:

"Marasmius oreades: a mushroom commonly found on lawns in summer and early autumn."

He let the book fall shut.

Outside, in the deep summer night, he lit a cigarette and smoked quietly.

A meteor fell across space, burning itself out quickly. The trees rustled softly.

The front door tapped shut.

Cynthia moved toward him in her robe.

"Can't sleep?"

"Too warm, I guess."

"It's not warm."

"No," he said, feeling his arms. "In fact, it's cold." He sucked on the cigarette twice, then,

121

not looking at her, said, "Cynthia . . . What if . . . ?" He snorted and had to stop. "Well, what if Roger was right this morning? Mrs. Goodbody, what if she's right, too? Something terrible *is* happening. Like—well—" he nodded at the sky and the million stars—"Earth being invaded by things from other worlds, maybe."

"Hugh!"

"No, let me run wild."

"It's quite obvious we're not being invaded or we'd notice."

"Let's say we've only half-noticed, become uneasy about something. What? How could we be invaded? By what means would creatures invade?"

Cynthia looked at the sky and was about to try something when he interrupted.

"No, not meteors or flying saucers. Not things we can see. What about bacteria? That comes from outer space, too, doesn't it?"

"I read once, yes—"

"Spores, seeds, pollens, viruses probably bombard our atmosphere by the billions every second and have done so for millions of years. Right now we're sitting out under an invisible rain. It falls all over the country, the cities, the towns, and right now . . . our lawn."

"*Our* lawn?"

"*And* Mrs. Goodbody's. But people like her are always pulling weeds, spraying poison, kicking toadstools off their grass. It would be hard for any strange life form to survive in cities. Weather's a problem, too. Best climate might be South: Alabama, Georgia, Louisiana. Back in the damp bayous, they could grow to a fine size."

But Cynthia was beginning to laugh now.

"Oh, really, you don't believe, do you, that this Great Bayou or whatever Greenhouse Novelty Company that sent Tom his package is owned and operated by six-foot-tall mushrooms from another planet?"

"If you put it that way, it sounds funny," he admitted.

"Funny! It's hilarious!" She threw her head back deliciously.

"Good grief!" he cried, suddenly irritated. "Something's going on! Mrs. Goodbody is rooting out and killing *marasmius oreades*. What is *marasmius oreades?* A certain kind of mushroom. Simultaneously, and I suppose you'll call it coincidence, by special delivery, what arrives the same day? Mushrooms for Tom! What else happens? Roger fears he may soon cease to be! Within hours, he vanishes, then telegraphs us, warning us not to accept what? The special delivery mushrooms for Tom! Has Roger's son got a similar package in the last few days? He has! Where do the packages come from? New Orleans! And where is Roger going when he vanishes? New Orleans! Do you see, Cynthia, do you see? I wouldn't be upset if all these separate things didn't lock together! Roger, Tom, Joe, mushrooms, Mrs. Goodbody, packages, destinations, everything in one pattern!"

She was watching his face now, quieter, but still amused. "Don't get angry."

"I'm not!" Fortnum almost shouted. And then he simply could not go on. He was afraid that if he did, he would find himself shouting with laughter, too, and somehow he did not want that. He stared at the surrounding houses up and down the block and thought of the dark cellars and the neighbor boys who read *Popular Mechanics* and sent their money in by the millions to raise the mushrooms hidden away. Just as he, when a boy, had mailed off for chemicals, seeds, turtles, numberless salves and sickish ointments. In how many million American homes tonight were billions of mushrooms rousing up under the ministrations of the innocent?

"Hugh?" His wife was touching his arm now. "Mushrooms, even big ones, can't think. They can't move. They don't have arms and legs. How could they run a mail-order service and 'take over' the world? Come on, now. Let's look at your terrible fiends and monsters!"

She pulled him toward the door. Inside, she headed for the cellar, but he stopped, shaking his head, a foolish smile shaping itself somehow to his mouth. "No, no, I know what we'll find. You win. The whole thing's silly. Roger will be back next week and we'll all get drunk together. Go on up to bed now and I'll drink a glass of warm milk and be with you in a minute . . . well, a couple of minutes . . ."

"That's better!" She kissed him on both cheeks, squeezed him, and went away up the stairs.

In the kitchen, he took out a glass, opened the refrigerator, and was pouring the milk when he stopped suddenly.

Near the front of the top shelf was a small yellow dish. It was not the dish that held his attention, however. It was what lay in the dish.

The fresh-cut mushrooms.

He must have stood there for half a minute, his breath frosting the refrigerated air, before he reached out, took hold of the dish, sniffed it, felt the mushrooms, then at last, carrying the dish, went out into the hall. He looked up the stairs, hearing Cynthia moving about in the bedroom, and was about to call up to her, "Cynthia, did you put *these* in the refrigerator!?"

Then he stopped. He knew her answer. She had not.

He put the dish of mushrooms on the newel at the bottom of the stairs and stood looking at them. He imagined himself, in bed later, looking at the walls, the open windows, watching the moonlight sift patterns on the ceiling.

He heard himself saying, Cynthia? And her answering, yes? And him saying, there *is* a way for mushrooms to grow arms and legs . . . What? she would say, silly, silly man, what? And he would gather courage against her hilarious reaction and go on, what if a man wandered through the swamp, picked the mushrooms, and *ate* them . . . ?

No response from Cynthia.

Once inside the man, would the mushrooms spread through his blood, take over every cell, and change the man from a man to a—Martian? Given this theory, would the mushroom *need* its own arms and legs? No, not when it could borrow people, live inside and become them. Roger ate mushrooms given him by his son. Roger became "something else." He kidnapped himself. And in one last flash of sanity, of being "himself," he telegraphed us, warning us not to accept the special delivery mushrooms. The "Roger" that telephoned later was no longer Roger but a captive of what he had eaten! Doesn't that figure, Cynthia? Doesn't it, doesn't it?

No, said the imagined Cynthia, no, it doesn't figure, no, no, no . . .

There was the faintest whisper, rustle, stir from the cellar. Taking his eyes from the bowl, Fortnum walked to the cellar door and put his ear to it.

"Tom?"

No answer.

"Tom, are you down there?"

No answer.

"Tom?"

After a long while, Tom's voice came up from below.

"Yes, Dad?"

"It's after midnight," said Fortnum, fighting to keep his voice from going high. "What are you doing down there?"

No answer.

"I said—"

"Tending to my crop," said the boy at last, his voice cold and faint.

"Well, get up out of there! You hear me?!"

Silence.

"Tom? Listen! Did you put some mushrooms in the refrigerator tonight? If so, why?"

Ten seconds must have ticked by before the boy replied from below. "For you and Mom to eat, of course."

Fortnum heard his heart moving swiftly, and had to take three deep breaths before he could go on.

"Tom? You didn't . . . that is . . . you haven't by any chance eaten some of the mushrooms yourself, have you?"

"Funny you ask that," said Tom. "Yes. To-night. On a sandwich after supper. Why?"

*　　*　　*

Fortnum held to the doorknob. Now it was his turn not to answer. He felt his knees beginning to melt and he fought the whole silly senseless fool thing. No reason, he tried to say, but his lips wouldn't move.

"Dad?" called Tom softly from the cellar. "Come on down." Another pause. "I want you to see the harvest."

Fortnum felt the knob slip in his sweaty hand. The knob rattled. He gasped.

"Dad?" called Tom softly.

Fortnum opened the door.

The cellar was completely black below.

He stretched his hand in toward the light switch. As if sensing this intrusion, from somewhere Tom said:

"Don't. Light's bad for the mushrooms."

Fortnum took his hand off the switch.

He swallowed. He looked back at the stair leading up to his wife. *I suppose,* he thought, *I should go say goodbye to Cynthia. But why should I think that! Why should I think that at* all? *No reason, is there!*

None.

"Tom?" he said, affecting a jaunty air. "Ready or not, here I come!"

And stepping down in darkness, he shut the door.

It's getting harder and harder to find a little peace and quiet these days.

THE INSTRUMENT

Martha Soukup

Melanie liked to go to the old thrift shop and lose herself among the shelves of worn bric-a-brac and the lumpy old furniture.

She would use her bus pass and take the noisy, jostling ride eleven long blocks up to the store. If she had time, sometimes she walked all the way home, through sidewalks as loud and jostling as the bus. Walking eleven blocks and then three flights up to the apartment helped tire her out, so she could get to sleep.

The thrift store wasn't the sort of place kids went. There usually weren't many adults there, either, and mostly those ignored her. Melanie could thumb through paperbacks published before she was born—or before her mother was born—and sort through shelves full of unmatched coffee mugs, reading the slogans and jokes printed on them.

Her favorite place was the basement. Almost no one went down there.

The basement was littered with the worst of the used furniture: sofas and tables people didn't buy for years even though they were marked at five or ten dollars, really ugly chairs in green and purple plaid with springs sticking up funny through the cushions, tables with cigarette holes burned in them. The basement smelled like dust and old plumbing leaks.

Sometimes Melanie would carry down an old paperback from upstairs and curl up on a grayish-gold plush sofa and read. She could still hear people walking around upstairs, and talking, and the rumbles of traffic outside. But if the book was good she could lose herself in it and ignore all that.

This day she poked around the corners of the basement looking for something interesting. She didn't have a lot of time. She had to be home by three so Mom could go buy groceries.

Some clerk had thrown together a bunch of musical instruments on a big dining table in back. They weren't the good ones, not that the thrift shop got anything that was very good. Even so, these were pretty beat up.

Melanie picked up a yellow plastic recorder, an instrument like a flute she knew was supposed to be made out of wood, and blew softly into the mouthpiece. It made a strangled little sound like a pigeon with asthma. She picked up a kid-size guitar missing two strings and strummed the remaining four, listening to the dull plinky throb of them.

There was a tambourine with a crack in its wooden frame, a rusty toy harmonica, and an empty violin case. Off to the side was a cheap electric organ with some keys broken off at one end. Melanie hit a bunch of keys with her finger, pretending she was making a melody, though it wasn't plugged in and all she heard was *thump thump thump.*

On top of the organ was the instrument.

It was a little bigger than a viola, but squarer, with a long blunt spike on the other end from the fingerboard, like she thought only cellos and basses were supposed to have. The pale goldish wood looked very old, dry, and worn, like it had sucked in all its varnish years ago from starvation, to survive.

It had no strings at all, and there was no bow.

Melanie picked it up and flicked her fingernail against the top of the instrument, near its curlicue soundholes. She expected a cracked dead sound.

Instead, the instrument sang with a low, deep resonance that went all the way from the bottom of her spine to the top of her scalp.

Melanie stood still, surprised. More carefully she tapped it again.

She could barely hear it, but the hum of the instrument made the tiny hairs on her arms tingle.

"Well, it's not broken after all," she said. "No strings and no bow, but it's not broken." Hearing her voice out loud startled her. She tapped the instrument a third time.

This time she noticed: When the vibrating belly of the instrument sounded, even in low answer to a tap, all other noises seemed to go away. It wasn't loud enough to drown them out, but it was *pure* enough to, somehow. No footsteps, no big truck sounds, no chatter of the clerks upstairs.

There was a tag tied to the fingerboard of the instrument. She turned it over to see the price. $11. Melanie emptied her pockets onto the dining table. She had three dollars and eighteen cents.

She took the instrument upstairs and showed it to the clerk at the cash register. "It doesn't have any strings or any bow," she said. "It doesn't work at all. Would you sell it for three dollars?"

The clerk, a woman with a lined forehead and pink lipstick, frowned. "I don't set the prices. If you're not going to buy it, you put it back."

Melanie took the instrument back into the basement and set it on the dining table. When

the table knocked it, she heard its hum, faintly. It looked very old and strange, valuable and worthless at the same time. She wanted to hear it really played.

She took it off the dining table and walked around the basement with it, looking for another place. There was a chipped and lopsided television stand behind a big chest of drawers. She put the instrument on its lower shelf. It wasn't really hidden. It wasn't cheating to put it there.

The bus home was full. She stood jammed between a guy wearing huge black boots and a fat woman holding two shopping bags from a department store. The guy in boots was listening to music on earphones, turned up so loud Melanie could hear fast tinny drumbeats buzzing out of them. The fat woman was chewing gum, *smack smack smack.* A bunch of kids in back shouted and laughed. The bus's engine roared when it started up after a stop. Motorcycles revved and cars were honking.

Melanie tried to remember what the instrument sounded like when she tapped on it in the basement of the thrift store. Everyone kept making too much noise.

"You're late," Mom said when Melanie put her key in the lock and opened the door.

"Sorry," Melanie said.

Addison and Brent were running around the

living room snapping towels at each other and yowling. Brent bumped into the table, and the lamp on it crashed to the floor. The lightbulb made a loud pop and went out.

"Boys, shut up!" Mom said. "Stop that. Melanie, change that bulb while I'm out."

"Okay," Melanie said.

"And check the baby. I think he needs changing."

Change bulb, change baby. Peter was hiccuping in a way that meant he was probably about to start wailing.

"I'll be back in two hours," Mom said. The door slammed behind her. You had to slam it to make it lock.

Addison, who was in third grade, had his towel wrapped around the neck of Brent, who was in second. "You broke the lamp, you broke the lamp!" he shouted.

"Ow!" howled Brent.

Melanie took the towels away. "Nobody broke the lamp. Watch television." The boys turned on a cartoon, listened for a while, turned up the volume. They weren't hitting each other, though.

Peter started wailing. Melanie got out a diaper.

Years and years ago she and Mom had lived in a house outside the city with Grandma and Grandpa. That was before there was Addison and before there was Brent. Way before there was Peter. She barely remembered. It was quiet in that house, and she had a room all to herself.

She finished putting the new diaper on Peter and took the stinky one into the hall to drop down the garbage chute. She couldn't hear the cartoons from there. She remembered the instrument. A lump formed in her throat when she remembered it, how quiet and peaceful it sounded. She didn't know why.

She didn't realize how long she'd stood at the garbage chute, leaning against the wall, until from far away she heard a crash.

"Mel!" said Brent. He was tugging her sleeve. "Addison broke all the lightbulbs! He said he'd change it and he stood on the kitchen counter to get the lightbulbs and he pulled them all out and they fell on the floor and he broke them and then he fell on the floor, too!"

Melanie blinked and remembered she was supposed to be watching the boys. "Oh, no," she said. She dropped the diaper down the chute and hurried after Brent.

Addison wasn't hurt. There were three bulbs not broken in the mess on the floor, scattered lightbulbs and napkin and tissue packages. She swept the glass carefully and threw it out, and used one of the good bulbs to change the one in the lamp.

Where can I get eight dollars? she was thinking. *Maybe nine dollars, with tax.*

Peter was crying again. She picked him up and walked him around. The television seemed to bother him. She walked Peter into the other room, the bedroom she shared with Addison and Brent, shaking him gently up and down, humming under her breath. One low hum. It was meant to be strange and peaceful, but it didn't work the same.

Finally she got Peter settled. The boys were engrossed in the football game, which apparently was close and required a lot of shouting to help their team win.

Melanie went into her bedroom. She had an old-fashioned piggy bank, on which she'd written "School Supply Money" with a marker. Sometimes Mom gave her some change from shopping, and she was supposed to save it for when she needed a fancier binder or something like that. But she could end up studying music in school in a couple of years, so that was okay.

She counted the coins while the boys watched television. The bank had $9.16 in it. She took it all out and put it in a sock.

That was Sunday, and during the week Melanie had to come straight home from school to pick up Peter from Mrs. Douglas downstairs, and watch the boys. She wanted to go back to the thrift store. She worried someone would find the instrument on its bottom shelf. Someone who would buy it on a whim and put it in a closet, and she'd never know what happened to it.

In class the other kids kept laughing and whispering, and Mr. Arriaga just kept talking and talking and talking until Melanie wanted to put her fingers in her ears.

At home the boys stomped around and shouted and the baby cried.

"Can I go out for an hour?" she asked when Mom got home from work on Wednesday.

"I need you here."

"Well, you wouldn't if you didn't get in a fight with Grandma and Grandpa and we could still live there." Melanie was mad. "They could babysit and I could go do things."

Mom's eyes got very narrow. "Your grandparents," she said, and stopped. Then she said, "Your grandparents weren't going to respect your father. It's up to them to apologize."

"It's not like they were wrong," said Melanie. "We're lucky when he sends the check. When he comes around acting nice to you, that's when we're unlucky."

Then she was sent to her room for the rest of the night, which ruled out going on the bus to the thrift store. It wasn't much good to be sent to her room, because it was the boys' room, too, and they slammed in and out of it until their bedtime, then whispered and poked at each other until they finally fell asleep.

Melanie felt for the sock full of coins under her pillow. She imagined what it would be like to hold the worn, warm instrument in her hands. She tried to imagine what it would sound like if she could really play it.

Finally it was Saturday.

She had to help clean the apartment all morning. As soon as she could, she ran out.

The thrift store was running a half-off sale on clothes. It was crowded on the ground floor. She pushed through all the adult bodies to the basement stairs.

The instrument was not on the television stand where she'd left it.

"No!" Melanie said. She had the sock full of money in her hand. Her cheeks were hot. It wasn't there.

But it was on the table with the broken tamborine and the other junk instruments.

Melanie felt foolish and relieved both together.

She checked the price tag. It still said $11. She took it upstairs and squeezed through the customers, clutching the instrument protectively to her chest. She counted out the money, exact change. The clerk put the instrument in a used paper bag, with paper handles, from a bookstore.

If someone on the busy bus stumbled into her when it braked, it could crush her instrument. So Melanie walked along the busy Saturday sidewalk, holding the bag very carefully in front of her. People kept brushing her as they went by, not paying attention to kids on the sidewalk. She held her breath each time.

Partway home was a tiny park around the corner from the main street. The park was nothing, just a couple of benches on a bit of scrubby grass. Melanie couldn't wait any longer. She turned into the little park, sat down, and took out the instrument.

It looked so odd, like a cello but smaller, more rectangular. It looked older than the Constitution. It looked very, very fragile.

It looked, really, like a piece of junk.

Melanie could hardly remember why she'd wanted it. She just remembered how much she'd wanted it.

She tapped its faded flat belly.

One moment she was surrounded by the sound of cars and people talking on the sidewalk and the snores of the man sleeping on the other bench in the park. The next moment she was caught wholly in the quiet hum of the instrument under her tap.

It only lasted a moment. The hum died down, drowned out again by horns and people and snoring.

She tapped on the instrument a few more times. It wasn't enough. This wasn't a drum, after all. It needed strings, and probably, she guessed, it needed a bow. Then it would be something. Then it would be what it promised.

Then it could make everything else go away but the music.

Melanie put the instrument back in the paper bag and walked the rest of the way home, slowly, thinking about strings and about bows.

"What's in the bag, what's in the bag?" asked Brent when she got home.

"None of your business," she said.

"What's in the bag?"

"Mom, tell Brent to stop bothering me."

Mom was in the kitchen stirring spaghetti sauce with a wooden spoon. "Don't bother your sister!" she called.

Melanie went in the bedroom and stood on the chair and put the bag on the top shelf of the closet, the one even Addison couldn't quite reach, standing on the chair on tiptoes. The boys pushed at each other trying to see what she'd been carrying. "It's just junk from the junk store," she said.

"Oh, come on!" shouted Addison. "Not fair!"

She didn't pay any attention. Strings, bow. Strings, bow.

At night she read the yellow pages under the

covers with a flashlight. "Musical Instruments—Retail" listed dozens of shops. Some
specialized in violins, and more said they sold
everything.

She memorized the address of a store with a
big ad. She could get there on two buses.

When the clock said it was three in the
morning, she crept out of the bedroom into the
living room. Mom was on the sofabed, breathing loudly in her sleep. The baby was asleep
beside her in his crib.

Mom's purse had four twenty-dollar bills in
it, along with a bunch of ones and fives. Melanie slid one of the twenties out, put the wallet
back in the purse. She crept back to the bedroom past her brothers' bed and got under the
covers. Her heart was beating fast. She didn't
go to sleep for a long time.

Sunday morning Mom had her stay with Peter
while she took the boys out shopping for shoes.
Peter kept crying. She took down the instrument and just looked at it. It had secrets. She
would find them out. It was important.

When she heard Mom's key in the lock, she
quickly put the instrument in some plastic
shopping bags, and put the bundle in the bag
from the thrift store.

"Peter's fine, I'm going to go out now,
okay?" She hoped Mom hadn't noticed the
money.

"Fine, dear, be back by dinner," Mom said. Mom looked tired and worried.

Melanie dashed out the door. She had the music store's address memorized. And the twenty-dollar bill in her pocket.

It took forty minutes to get to the store. The store was big. There were guitars hanging on the walls, and keyboards on stands, and flutes and saxophones in cases, and racks of sheet music.

"Can I help you?" asked a man with a blond ponytail.

"I want to buy some strings," Melanie said.

"What kind of strings?"

"For this," she said. She felt she shouldn't show the instrument to anyone, but she couldn't see any way not to. She pulled it out of the bag.

"Where did you get that?" said the man.

"In a junk store." Melanie tried to sound casual. She didn't want him to know how important it was. It was hers.

"I've never seen an instrument like that," said the man. He reached out for it. She pulled it away. "I could put some violin strings on it," he said. "Maybe viola, for its size."

"You know how to put them on?" she asked.

"That part's straightforward," said the man. "What I don't know is how to tune it, since I don't know how it's supposed to be tuned. I could just tune it like a viola, if you wanted."

143

"How much would it cost?" Melanie asked.

He looked at her. "How much do you have?" he asked.

She got the idea that strings cost more than she knew. "Twenty dollars," she said.

"Well, with labor, putting the strings on and tuning—"

It made her nervous to think of someone else plucking the strings. "Don't tune it," she said, "just put them on. I'll tune it."

"*Well*, then," the man said, smiling at her. "If I don't have to tune it, it'll be cheaper. I can do it for you for ten dollars."

That was half her money. She thought he was selling the strings to her cheaper than their price, too. But there was nothing to do. "Okay," she said.

The man opened a drawer and took out some cardboard envelopes with metal strings in them. Melanie watched him put them on her instrument. She hated watching him touch it, but was fascinated to see the strings go on, twined around themselves to hold, wrapped around the pegs.

"You sure you don't want me to tune this?" he said, reaching to pluck a string.

"No!" Melanie said. "I know how to do it," she added quickly.

"Will that be all?" the man asked.

"A violin bow," she said. "Or a viola bow I guess. How much does that cost?"

"Well, that's a little more," he said. "I could sell you one of those for $29.95."

Her heart sank. Even with ten dollars left she needed another twenty. She'd never get that. Her mother would catch her.

"Please give me my instrument," she said. She gave the man the money for the strings and left the store, upset.

She got a seat on the bus and held the bag in her lap. The instrument hummed through its strings. It almost made her forget her stop. She had to jump up and excuse herself all the way to the door, protecting the instrument.

When she was almost home, she thought of something. There were a bunch of pawnshops on her street. They always had musical instruments in their windows. Maybe someone had pawned a bow. Maybe she could get one for ten dollars.

"I got a violin and it's got a bow," said the pawnshop man, "but you can't just buy the bow, you got to buy the violin."

"How much?" asked Melanie.

"Good violin," said the pawnshop man. "Ninety-five bucks."

"Can I try it?" said Melanie.

"You be careful or it's trouble," said the

145

pawnshop man. He frowned, but he handed her the violin and bow.

Melanie put the violin under her chin the way she'd seen on television and pulled the bow along its strings. It made a high ugly squeal. She winced. She put the violin on the counter.

She didn't put down the bow.

Inside its shopping bags, she could *feel* the instrument. Waiting.

"Can I just try the bow on my instrument?" she said.

"Well—"

She took out the instrument. She tightened its pegs until they felt right. What if it squealed like the violin? Then she sat on the floor, holding it upright in front of her like a cello, and she pulled the bow across it.

There was a long low sound so perfect that everything went away.

She didn't even know her arm was still moving, but the sound kept playing.

Perfect.

The instrument wanted to play forever and ever.

And ever.

And ever.

And it was dark and her arm slipped and the music stopped and the pawnshop man said, "Hey, what are you doing, give that here!"

The Instrument

He grabbed for her.

There were a whole bunch of people in the front of the store, shaking their heads, like they'd come inside over the course of hours, and just stood stuck once they got there. It was dark outside, the streetlights on.

Melanie didn't plan. She ducked away from the pawnshop man and ran toward the door, holding the instrument and bow up over her head out of harm's way. The pawnshop man, a big fat guy, got caught up in the knot of people as she ran between them. "What happened?" she heard them saying.

She ran down the sidewalk and around the corner and up an alley.

The instrument was so perfect, it was magic. Somehow she'd known it all along. She didn't know where it came from, but she would never give it up. It was worth everything. It was worth her whole life.

She squeezed through the locked, warped back gate of someone's backyard, off the alley, protecting the instrument with her body. She hid herself in the shadows under their back stairs.

She took up the bow and started to play.

The music played, and played, and played, until she heard everything, until she didn't hear anything.

And that's where they found her, the next

morning, the people in the apartment house, bow in her hand, fingers clutched around the instrument, all its strings snapped, quite, quite cold and still.

As quiet as no living thing could ever be.

A triumphant smile on her face.

Billy Sleator and I were once guests at a conference about scary stories. The organizer had asked us each to bring a new tale to read aloud in the dark. I'll never forget sitting in that hushed room and listening as Billy read this spine-tingling yarn. Part of me wanted to clobber him, because the story was so cool and I hadn't written it myself. But I also felt a delicious shiver of fear. Which is why I am very happy to be able to share it with you now. Even if I didn't write it.

THE ELEVATOR

William Sleator

It was an old building with an old elevator—a very small elevator, with a maximum capacity of three people. Martin, a thin twelve-year-old, felt nervous in it from the first day he and his father moved into the apartment. Of course he was always uncomfortable in elevators, afraid that they would fall, but there was something especially unpleasant about this one. Perhaps its baleful atmosphere was due to the light from the single fluorescent ceiling strip, bleak and dim on the dirty brown walls. Perhaps the problem was the door, which never stayed open quite long enough, and slammed shut with such ominous, clanging finality. Perhaps it was the way the mechanism shuddered in a kind of exhaustion each time it left a floor, as though it might never reach the next one. Maybe it was simply the dimensions of the contraption that bothered him, so small that it felt uncomfortably crowded even when there was only one other person in it.

Coming home from school the day after they moved in, Martin tried the stairs. But they were almost as bad, windowless, shadowy, with several dark landings where the lightbulbs had burned out. His footsteps echoed behind him like slaps on the cement, as though there was another person climbing, getting closer. By the time he reached the seventeenth floor, which seemed to take forever, he was winded and gasping.

His father, who worked at home, wanted to know why he was so out of breath. "But why didn't you take the elevator?" he asked, frowning at Martin when he explained about the stairs. *Not only are you skinny and weak and bad at sports,* his expression seemed to say, *but you're also a coward.* After that, Martin forced himself to take the elevator. He would have to get used to it, he told himself, just the way he got used to being bullied at school, and always picked last when they chose teams. The elevator was an undeniable fact of life.

He didn't get used to it. He remained tense in the trembling little box, his eyes fixed on the numbers over the door that blinked on and off so haltingly, as if at any moment they might simply give up. Sometimes he forced himself to look away from them, to the Emergency Stop button, or the red Alarm button. What would happen if he pushed one of them? Would a bell ring? Would the elevator stop between floors? And if it did, how would they get him out?

That was what he hated about being alone on the thing—the fear of being trapped there for hours by himself. But it wasn't much better when there were other passengers. He felt too close to any other rider, too intimate. And he was always very conscious of the effort people made *not* to look at one another, staring fixedly at nothing. Being short, in this one situation, was an advantage, since his face was below the eye level of adults, and after a brief glance they ignored him.

Until the morning the elevator stopped at the fourteenth floor, and the fat lady got on. She wore a threadbare green coat that ballooned around her; her ankles bulged above dirty sneakers. As she waddled into the elevator, Martin was sure he felt it sink under her weight. She was so big that she filled the cubicle; her coat brushed against him, and he had to squeeze into the corner to make room for her—there certainly wouldn't have been room for another passenger. The door slammed quickly behind her. And then, unlike everyone else she did not stand facing the door. She stood with her back to the door, wheezing, staring directly at Martin.

For a moment he met her gaze. Her features seemed very small, squashed together by the loose, fleshy mounds of her cheeks. She had no chin, only a great swollen mass of neck, barely contained by the collar of her coat. Her sparse red hair was pinned back by a plastic barrette. And her blue eyes, though tiny, were sharp and penetrating, boring into Martin's face.

Abruptly he looked away from her to the numbers over the door. She didn't turn around. Was she still looking at him? His eyes slipped back to hers, then quickly away. She was still watching him. He wanted to close his eyes; he wanted to turn around and stare into the corner, but how could he? The elevator creaked down to twelve, down to eleven. Martin looked at his watch; he looked at the numbers again. They weren't even down to nine yet. And then, against his will, his eyes slipped back to her face. She was still watching him. Her nose tilted up;

there was a large space between her nostrils and her upper lip, giving her a piggish look. He looked away again, clenching his teeth, fighting the impulse to squeeze his eyes shut against her.

She had to be crazy. Why else would she stare at him this way? What was she going to do next?

She did nothing. She only watched him, breathing audibly, until the elevator reached the first floor at last. Martin would have rushed past her to get out, but there was no room. He could only wait as she turned—reluctantly, it seemed to him—and moved so slowly out into the lobby. And then he ran. He didn't care what she thought. He ran past her, outside into the fresh air, and he ran almost all the way to school. He had never felt such relief in his life.

He thought about her all day. Did she live in the building? He had never seen her before, and the building wasn't very big—only four apartments on each floor. It seemed likely that she didn't live there, and had only been visiting somebody.

But if she were only visiting somebody, why was she leaving the building at seven thirty in the morning? People didn't make visits at that time of day. Did that mean she *did* live in the building? If so, it was likely—it was a certainty—that sometime he would be riding with her on the elevator again.

He was apprehensive as he approached the building after school. In the lobby, he considered the stairs. But that was ridiculous. Why should he be afraid of an old lady? If he was afraid of her, if he let it control him, then he was worse than all the names they called him at school. He pressed the button; he stepped into the empty elevator. He stared at the lights, urging the elevator on. It stopped on three.

At least it's not fourteen, he told himself; *the person she was visiting lives on fourteen.* He watched the door slide open—revealing a green coat, a piggish face, blue eyes already fixed on him as though she knew he'd be there.

It wasn't possible. It was like a nightmare. But there she was, massively real. "Going up!" he said, his voice a humiliating squeak.

She nodded, her flesh quivering, and stepped on. The door slammed. He watched her pudgy hand move toward the buttons. She pressed, not fourteen, but eighteen, the top floor, one floor above his own. The elevator trembled and began its ascent. The fat lady watched him.

He knew she had gotten on at fourteen this morning. So why was she on three, going up to eighteen now? The only floors *he* ever went to were seventeen and one. What was she doing? Had she been waiting for him? Was she riding with him on purpose?

But that was crazy. Maybe she had a lot of friends in the building. Or else she was a cleaning lady who worked in different apartments.

That had to be it. He felt her eyes on him as he stared at the numbers slowly blinking on and off—slower than usual, it seemed to him. Maybe the elevator was having trouble because of how heavy she was. It was supposed to carry three adults, but it was old. What if it got stuck between floors? What if it fell?

They were on five now. It occurred to him to press seven, get off there, and walk the rest of the way. And he would have done it, if he could have reached the buttons. But there was no room to get past her without squeezing against her, and he could not bear the thought of any physical contact with her. He concentrated on being in his room. He would be home soon, only another minute or so. He could stand anything for a minute, even this crazy lady watching him.

Unless the elevator got stuck between floors. Then what would he do? He tried to push the thought away, but it kept coming back. He looked at her. She was still staring at him, no expression at all on her squashed little features.

When the elevator stopped on his floor, she barely moved out of the way. He had to inch past her, rubbing against her horrible scratchy coat, terrified the door would close before he made it through. She quickly turned and watched him as the door slammed shut. And he thought, *Now she knows I live on seventeen.*

"Did you ever notice a strange fat lady on the elevator?" he asked his father that evening.

"Can't say as I have," he said, not looking away from the television.

He knew he was probably making a mistake, but he had to tell somebody. "Well, she was on the elevator with me twice today. And the funny thing was, she just kept staring at me, she never stopped looking at me for a minute. You think . . . you know of anybody who has a weird cleaning lady or anything?"

"What are you so worked up about now?" his father said, turning impatiently away from the television.

"I'm not worked up. It was just funny the way she kept staring at me. You know how people never look at each other in the elevator. Well, she just kept looking at me."

"What am I going to do with you, Martin?" his father said. He sighed and shook his head. "Honestly, now you're afraid of some poor old lady."

"I'm not afraid."

"You're afraid," said his father, with total assurance. "When are you going to grow up and act like a man? Are you going to be timid all your life?"

He managed not to cry until he got to his room—but his father probably knew he was crying anyway. He slept very little.

And in the morning, when the elevator door opened, the fat lady was waiting for him.

She was expecting him. She knew he lived on seventeen. He stood there, unable to move, and then backed away. And as he did so, her expression changed. She smiled as the door slammed.

He ran for the stairs. Luckily, the unlit flight on which he fell was between sixteen and fifteen. He only had to drag himself up one and a half flights with the terrible pain in his leg. His father was silent on the way to the hospital, disappointed and annoyed at him for being such a coward and a fool.

It was a simple fracture. He didn't need a wheelchair, only a cast and crutches. But he was condemned to the elevator now. Was that why the fat lady had smiled? Had she known it would happen this way?

At least his father was with him on the elevator on the way back from the hospital. There was no room for the fat lady to get on. And even if she did, his father would see her, he would realize how peculiar she was, and then maybe he would understand. And once they got home, he could stay in the apartment for a few days—the doctor had said he should use the leg as little as possible. A week, maybe—a whole week without going on the elevator. Riding up with his father, leaning on his crutches, he looked around the little cubicle and felt a kind of triumph. He had beaten the elevator, and the fat lady, for the time being. And the end of the week was very far away.

"Oh, I almost forgot," his father reached out his hand and pressed nine.

"What are you doing? You're not getting off, are you?" he asked him, trying not to sound panicky.

"I promised Terry Ullman I'd drop in on her," his father said, looking at his watch as he stepped off.

"Let me go with you. I want to visit her, too," Martin pleaded, struggling forward on his crutches.

But the door was already closing. "Afraid to be on the elevator alone?" his father said, with a look of total scorn. "Grow up, Martin." The door slammed shut.

Martin hobbled to the buttons and pressed nine, but it didn't do any good. The elevator stopped at ten, where the fat lady was waiting for him. She moved in quickly; he was too slow, too unsteady on his crutches to work his way past her in time. The door sealed them in; the elevator started up.

"Hello, Martin," she said, and laughed, and pushed the Stop button.

*Scary comes in many different flavors. Being
chased by a monster is scary. Walking alone
in the dark is scary. And sometimes scary
happens in broad daylight, when the world
turns unexpectedly strange and you
have to make a choice.
I think that may be the scariest thing of all.*

THE PACKET

Nina Kiriki Hoffman

"I bet it's space food," said Rikki. "Like the
astronauts eat." She squeezed the opaque silvery
sausage-shaped packet between her fingers, peer-
ing through the oval plastic window in the middle at the brownish-red contents. She had found
the hand-sized packet under her pillow that
morning when she woke up, and brought it to
show her friend Arnold on their way to school.

"Camping food," said Arnold. "Yuck. Some
weekends I have to spend with my dad, he
takes me camping. We have to eat stuff out of
plastic things like that. It's yucky." He spat on

the asphalt next to the front tire of his bike. "You should just toss it."

Rikki slanted a look at Arnold, then glanced up at old Mrs. Revel's front yard, where green sword iris leaves cleft the morning breeze, and beyond, to the twisted pepper tree. Ragged lawn stretched between the house, the pepper willow, and the iris beds, reaching to touch other clumps of flowers not yet blooming.

Rikki wished old Mrs. Revel was rocking on her porch the way she always was in the afternoons, so Rikki could show her the packet and ask her about it. But Mrs. Revel was never on her porch before school started.

"Toss it, Rikki," Arnold said again. "Who knows where it came from?" Lately, Arnold had gotten scared of germs. His mother made him wash his hands so much that now he did it on his own all the time. It made him less fun to play with; he was afraid to touch things he used to love, like salamanders and worms. He didn't like sharing food or drinks anymore, either.

"You just wish *you* had found it," said Rikki. Last night's dream touched her mind, then ran away, as if she were now It in a game of tag. She frowned. "If I throw it away you'll take it." She slid her arms out of her backpack straps and unzipped the outer pocket. She tucked the silver thing away safe, zipped the pocket, then forgot about it.

Later that afternoon while they were studying math, chalk scritched and squeaked on the blackboard as their sixth grade teacher, Mr. Clifton, wrote out fractions problems. Through the open window, bees droned in the lilac bushes. The warmth of the spring afternoon and the heavy smell of the flowers made it hard to concentrate.

Rikki was still mad because the cafeteria lunch had had chocolate pudding for dessert and Arnold wouldn't share his. Her father never put desserts in her sack lunch. She fished her pack out from under her chair and touched the cat face stitched on its pink-and-blue back. It was like all the stuff her mom sent her since the divorce, sweetly cute, like the dolls with their dumb faces and frilly dresses, not a decent G.I. Joe action figure in the bunch. Mom didn't understand that what Rikki really wanted was camo clothes and Supersoakers that looked like real guns. Rikki told Mom, and Mom just smiled and didn't hear.

Dad made Rikki use the cat-face backpack anyway. He said it was a perfectly good pack no matter how dumb it looked.

Arnold, sitting next to her, nudged her foot with his sneaker. She glanced at him. He nodded toward the board. For math tests, Mr. Clifton put three problems up on the board, gave you five minutes, then erased them and put the next set up. She'd missed the first set, fallen asleep with her eyes open thinking about Arnold's treachery and Mom's selective deafness. Rikki sighed and fumbled in her pack for a pencil.

Her fingers touched the silver packet. It felt warm and gooshy. Was she right? Was it space food? She wondered what it would smell like if she opened it. Her father left food in containers in the refrigerator a long time. You never knew what you'd find when you opened the containers. Mostly different kinds of stinky mold, dull green or gray or black. Not reddish-brown.

She stared into her backpack and turned the packet until she could see the oval window.

Something inside had changed.

Arnold kicked her again.

She got out a pencil and worked on math problems, and all the time, something strange tingled under her mind, whispering, "I'm here, I'm here, just wait'll you get a chance to think, just wait, I'm here. . . ."

After school she hid in the girls' bathroom until she was sure Arnold had left. He had a bike and she walked to school, but they usually traveled together anyway—he rode very slowly, or she ran for short stretches. They lived across the street from each other. At one time Rikki had hoped her dad would marry Arnold's mother, but she'd given up on the idea since they had gotten into sixth grade and Arnold turned out to be such a weirdo about germs. She didn't want a brother who was such a dork. It was risky enough having a *friend* who was such a dork.

But she'd known him forever, and he was her comrade in battle, and he stuck up for her when no one else did. Same way she stuck up for him.

Only, today she wanted to be alone with the packet. She had already heard what Arnold had to say about the packet, and now she wanted it to herself.

When she was sure he would be gone, she slipped out of the bathroom and headed for the school's back door, which led to the playground. She looked around. A couple kids tossing a softball. No Arnold.

She crossed the asphalt and the lawn and went to her favorite climbing tree, climbed up about five feet, and settled in the place where she always thought she would build a nest if she were a bird, even though it wasn't very high. Three branches grew out from the trunk almost side by side and made a good secure sitting place. Sometimes she played lookout up there.

Today, Rikki got the packet out of her backpack.

It was warm.

Through the window in the packet, she saw two staring yellow eyes.

With a shriek that would have disqualified her from the Junior Green Berets, she dropped the packet. It tumbled to the packed earth below, making a plopping sound, with just a tiny hint of snap.

Her dream swam back into her mind.

"Just for you," said the thing with the silver suit and the funny voice. "All for you." And it handed her a big present wrapped in silver paper, with a big red bow on it that had lots of loops and curly ends, and she knew it was the best present ever, and not even her birthday. "Be careful!" said the thing. "Take good care!" It waved goodbye, not really smiling—its lips weren't made for smiling—and flew out the window.

And when she woke up, she had found the packet under her pillow. She thought maybe Daddy had put it there. Sometimes he sneaked into her room and left little presents, especially if he had gotten good tips at the restaurant the day before. But he hadn't had his special secret smile at breakfast that morning, so she didn't say anything about what the Present Fairy had left. Besides, what could she say about a thing that looked like *that?*

Sitting up in the tree with her backpack perched on her knees, Rikki listened to the quiet. During recess, kids would be everywhere—playing dodgeball and four-square on the asphalt, tossing basketballs at the two rusty hoops, running across the lawn, playing on the jungle gym and the swings. Times like that she just knew there was no place to be alone, even if she wanted to be. She could act as a lookout in her tree, but everyone could see her, too.

Now, with that *thing* on the ground below her, Rikki listened for a single other human sound.

The kids playing softball had left. She couldn't see anyone at all. Traffic hummed beyond the school, stop and start and stop.

She heard a little sliding sound from the packet, and a tiny, locked-in-a-box wail.

Rikki could feel her heart pounding. It pulsed in her ears, a sound and a feeling. She set her pack beside her on a branch and leaned forward until she could see the ground between her knees.

The packet lay there, wriggling. "Meep. Meeeep." A tiny scrunchy face peered out at her through the window. The packet rolled over. It was coming toward the tree.

Maybe it was like a big spider or a wasp. If you thought about it you'd be too scared to do anything about it, but if you just hauled off and stomped it, or slapped it to death with a book right away, that took care of it.

Except Rikki had tried smashing a wasp last summer and it took three swats to kill it. She had felt more horrible with each swat. A good soldier killed right away so the killee didn't have to suffer.

"Meeeeeeeep," wailed the little lost voice. The packet lay on the ground, twitching.

Rikki grabbed her backpack, then crept along one of the branches and dropped to the ground beyond the packet, and ran and ran and ran, never stopping till she was safe on Mrs. Revel's front porch.

"Lemonade, dear?" said Mrs. Revel, pouring a tall glassful from a large plastic pitcher. She crumpled a mint leaf from a plate of them and dropped it in. "My, you're out of breath. And young Arnold has already come and gone. What's the matter, Rikki?"

"There was—there—" Rikki took a long sip of lemonade. Her cheeks were so hot she felt she could heat a house, and she was sweating her dark hair to her head. "M-M-Mrs. Revel?"

"What, dear?"

"It was a . . ." She thought of the packet on the ground, twitching and crying. What could she say about it? What difference did it make? Maybe someone else would take it home or throw it away, maybe it would melt in the rain, maybe it would just lie there. It wasn't her problem anymore. And there were some things grown-ups, even Mrs. Revel, just wouldn't understand. "I don't know," she said.

Mrs. Revel leaned forward in her rocker, her black eyes as bright as steely marbles in the sun. "Rikki, dear," she said.

"It was just this thing, a little ugly thing I left on the playground. It doesn't matter anymore, okay?"

"What sort of thing? Was it yours? Did you take it from somebody else, dear?"

Rikki flushed. She kept hoping everybody would forget about that stupid stuffed bear. That was in fourth grade, anyway, and Lisa Calvert said it was okay when she got it back, even though one eye had come off.

"It was mine! I found it in my room this morning."

"Are you sure, honey?"

Rikki gulped down her lemonade, slammed the glass onto the table, and ran straight across the yard, crunching some of the iris leaves on the way, ignoring Mrs. Revel's cries of "Rikki! Rikki!" which sounded like "Meep! Meep!" as she got farther away.

At home she ignored the television and got out her homework. It was hard to *not* think about three things at once. Mrs. Revel's betrayal, the packet, and Lisa Calvert's teddy bear kept swimming through her social studies book. By the time Daddy got home, she was thoroughly upset and hadn't gotten anything done. He was in one of his low-tip grumps, talking about college money, so Rikki didn't say anything to him at all.

She went to bed with the cold leftover pizza

they'd had for dinner lying like a lump in her stomach.

That night she dreamed again. The thing in the silver suit came back, and even though its mouth wasn't made for frowning, she could tell it was mad. "Bad!" it said. "Not careful! Do better. For you, for all you." Its voice sounded like a bee and a fly buzzing at the same time.

Then it looked sad, its big yellow eyes pinching half shut. It touched her hair with a three-fingered hand. "Do better," it said, "please."

When she woke up, the silver packet lay on the rug below the window. It moaned. This time it said, "Help."

She sat on her bed, pulling the covers tight around her, and looked at the packet. No matter how close she held the covers, she felt cold. Wasps and spiders didn't say "help."

After all, it was still inside the packet and couldn't seem to get out. She slipped out of bed and crept closer.

A little face pressed against the packet's window. It reminded Rikki of the thing in her dream. A tiny hand came up and scratched at the packet window with three fingers. "Help. Help."

Rikki got up and went to the closet, where, after shoving aside a stack of *Mad* magazines, she unearthed a doll bed her mother had sent her for Christmas. It was big enough for the life-size preemie baby doll Mom had sent along with it. The doll was still in its plastic-windowed box somewhere behind Rikki's winter shoes.

She put the doll bed on the rug beside the packet, then sat on her heels a minute. Good soldiers had courage. They faced unpleasant duties with fortitude. She folded back the blanket in the doll bed, then, biting her lower lip, picked up the packet between finger and thumb. It was still warm, and not quite as gooshy as it had been. There were angles and hard things in it now. The tiny voice cried, "Ye! Ye!" It sounded happy.

Rikki put it in the doll bed and lowered the blanket over it. There was a tiny, terrified scream. Rikki bit her lip and folded the blanket back, exposing the window in the packet. Yellow eyes stared up at her, then blinked. "Help," said the thing in the packet. It sounded hopeless now.

Rikki shivered. She put the doll bed carefully on the dresser. Then she got her school clothes and went to the bathroom to change, where the thing in the packet couldn't see her.

At breakfast Daddy had the radio on. "All communications to and from the South American country of Colombia have ceased. Authorities are investigating. AP reports a sudden cessation in telephone and Internet communications with

Norway. Satellite infrared pictures show startling anomalies. Other information shortfalls from . . ."

Daddy growled and switched the radio to an oldies station. Rikki ate her cereal and wondered what to do about the thing upstairs. What if she let it out and it turned out to be like Stripe in the movie *Gremlins,* an evil creature that might kill Daddy? Maybe she should microwave it before she let it out.

"So Happy Together" ended, and an announcer came on the radio. "This just in," he said. He sounded upset.

"Something hit Afghanistan. Nobody knows what. I mean, they're saying that everyone in the country is dead, and they can't figure out how. Maybe it's just a rumor, how could we know about it if everybody was dead? But someone is reporting this. I mean—" Then another announcer came on and said the first one was just fooling.

"Irresponsible nitwits," said Daddy, and changed the station again. But there was talking on all the stations. Daddy turned the radio off. "Honey? It's time to go to school, isn't it?"

Rikki looked at the clock. "Oh. Yeah," she said. She got the lunch he had packed for her out of the refrigerator (if the cafeteria lunches had pudding again today, she'd hit Arnold until he gave her his) and stuffed it in her backpack.

Arnold was waiting for her outside. He gave

her a mean glare. "So where were you yesterday, huh?"

"I had to stay after."

"Sure. Why?"

"Math," she said. "I missed too many problems on the test."

"Liar. Mr. Clifton couldn't grade the tests till last night. Anyway, he doesn't make people stay after school, he just gives them extra homework. Where were you really?"

"I was in the bathroom. I felt sick."

He frowned at her a minute, then started off, pedaling faster than she could walk. "You missed the big war, anyway!" he yelled over his shoulder.

That was right. She was supposed to be one of his soldiers in the trench warfare they were staging with the boys a block over. There was a big vacant lot with holes in the ground where someone had planned to build a mall and someone else had stopped it, and they staged battles there, sometimes three times a week. As long as Rikki got home in time to do laundry before Daddy got home so he couldn't see all the mud on her clothes, everything was okay.

Arnold had started wearing rubber gloves to war, but no one had noticed yet but Rikki, so it was okay.

"I'm sorry!" she yelled at Arnold's retreating back.

"I lost!" he yelled, and pedaled away.

Now he would be grumpy for a week. There was nobody like Arnold for bearing a grudge.

In current events Grady said six countries had disappeared since the day before.

Arnold told him not to be stupid.

Rikki glanced at Mr. Clifton. The teacher looked pale. He was chewing on his mustache.

"I heard about some countries disappearing on the radio," Rikki said, "but I thought it was a joke. Mr. Clifton?" Rikki hoped she'd get a good mark for participation in current events.

"I don't know what to believe," said Mr. Clifton. He looked sick.

After current events, they had English, then recess. Rikki noticed she was sweating a lot. When she got outside she felt even worse. Something was happening to the weather. The air was hot and smelled bad, and it was hard to breathe. Sun fried down from the sky as though it had moved closer to the Earth and wanted to cook everyone. No one ran on the playground; everyone sat around trying to breathe, and as soon as the bell rang and they went back inside, the principal announced over the public address system that school was closing due to an air quality emergency.

Rikki wished there was a bus to take her

home, even though she only lived four blocks away. Her breathing was hoarse. Her throat hurt. She dropped her pack somewhere on the way home from school, and she didn't even care. She had her house key; that was all that mattered. She crawled the last half-block home and drank three glasses of water from the kitchen sink. The water tasted like hot metal.

She crawled on her hands and knees upstairs and into her room.

And there on the dresser, in the full light of the midday sun, lay the doll bed. Rikki ran to it and took it into the shade.

She sat on the floor and looked at the creature in the packet. Its eyes were shut and it looked boiled. She had caught pollywogs the spring before and put them in a fishbowl on the windowsill, and they all died from too much heat, Daddy told her. "I'm sorry, I'm sorry, I'm sorry," she whispered to the thing in the packet, because a good soldier didn't torture captives, even if they were Nazis or evil gremlins.

"Help." It was only a thread of sound.

Rikki listened to her own labored breathing, waiting for the tiny word to come again, but it didn't. She got her nail scissors from the bedside table and snipped the packet open at the top, after she felt it to make sure there weren't any little arms or legs in the way.

For a long time nothing happened except a little wet smelly stuff came out the end of the packet and stained one of the doll blankets greenish yellow. Then, with tiny twitches, the creature pulled itself out of the packet. It had two long skinny arms and two short stubby legs. Two three-fingered hands. One bald head, two big yellow eyes, a scrunchy little bump-nosed face with a slit for a mouth. It looked almost like a tiny human, but partly like an elf. Mostly it looked like the thing in her dream. It was pale, wrinkled, and damp, and it lay curled in its own wetness like a little dead animal in a jar. Then it lifted its matchstick arms, twitched its tiny hands, and said, "Help."

"Help, what help? What do you want, any-way?" Rikki asked. A tear ran down her nose and landed next to the thing. It flinched away.

"Water? You want water? Or what? Food? Don't you know any other words? What are you, any-way?" The tightness in her chest was easing. Rikki took a deep breath. The air tasted better than it had all morning, and she didn't feel too hot anymore.

The thing opened and closed a hand as small as a hummingbird's claw. Rikki bit her lip and leaned down to study the creature. One of its legs looked broken, bent in a bad, swollen place below the knee. Maybe that had happened when she dropped it from the tree. She rubbed her eyes to get rid of the tears and whispered, "I'm sorry" again.

"Help." It sounded stronger now.

"What do you *want?*" she said. "I can't fix a broken bone."

Its arms flailed. She held out her index finger to it, and it reached up and gripped her, with arms and legs. It was warm and wet and it smelled bad. She wondered if it would start eating her now. But it just hugged her finger and closed its yellow eyes and, even though its mouth wasn't made for smiling, it smiled.

Then it melted. She didn't see it go; it was hanging on her finger, and then it was just a wetness, and then it was gone, and there was a silver diamond-shaped patch on the back of her hand that wouldn't come off.

Her leg hurt. She pulled up her jeans and looked at her leg, and saw a dark red ring around her calf. It hurt. It hurt really bad.

She thought about sitting in a closet hanging on to Lisa Calvert's teddy bear. Lisa had brought the bear to school to show-and-tell, and left it on the counter by the hamster cage, and then when they got back from recess it was gone.

It was right after Mom had left. Rikki had a stuffed turtle and a stuffed tiger of her own, but somehow Lisa's teddy bear seemed more important than anything Rikki had. Lisa's mom still lived at home. So Rikki had taken the teddy bear home in her backpack. She hid in the closet with the bear and hugged it, hoping something would come from the bear, some feeling that maybe the world would stay all right.

Instead she just felt bad, especially when she thought about everyone at school asking everyone else what had happened to Lisa's bear.

Rikki brought the bear back the next day. She had tried to sneak it back to the counter she had taken it from, but Mrs. Peterson came in and found her, and there were a lot of horrible questions asked, and her life was miserable for weeks after that.

Now she looked at the doll bed, the deflated silver packet, the wet green-brown stain. Her leg throbbed, but she felt good. Air tasted sweet, and the horrible pressing-down heat of the morning was gone.

A prisoner of war had asked for help, and she had finally figured out what help to give.

It would be all right now.

Maybe. How many kids like her in different countries would know how to take care of something scary in a silver packet?

How many other kids knew how to stomp wasps?

ABOUT THE AUTHORS

ROBERT J. HARRIS is the designer of the best-selling fantasy board game *Talisman*. His hobbies are gaming, fencing, and playing blues harmonica. He and his wife, fantasy novelist Deborah Turner Harris, live in St. Andrews, Scotland, with their sons Matthew, Robert, and Jamie.

NEAL SHUSTERMAN is the author of many award-winning novels, including *The Eyes of Kid Midas* and *What Daddy Did* (both ALA Best Books). His short-story collections include *Darkness Creeping* and *MindStorms*. He lives in Southern California with his wife, Elaine, and their two sons.

JEREMY SABACEK is a seventeen-year-old high school student who lives in Vestal, New York with his parents and younger brother Brent. He enjoys drawing, especially cartooning; reading science fiction and fantasy books; and watching and discussing movies.

About the Authors

STEVE RASNIC TEM is the author of more than two hundred horror, science fiction, and mystery short stories. His work has appeared in magazines like *Isaac Asimov's Science Fiction Magazine* and anthologies such as *A Nightmare's Dozen* and *100 Wicked Little Witches*. He has been nominated for the Bram Stoker and Philip K. Dick awards, among others.

MICHAEL MARKIEWICZ's stories have appeared in several of Bruce Coville's anthologies. Michael lives in rural Pennsylvania with his wife, Lois Rebekah, and their two beagles, Nickel and Penny.

JAMES REEVES (1909–1978) is one of the best-loved children's poets of the twentieth century. He published over twenty-five collections of poetry and short stories, including *The Wandering Moon*, *The Blackbird in the Lilac* and *Pigeons and Princesses*, and was a Fellow of the Royal Society of Literature.

RAY BRADBURY is beloved throughout the world as one of the most poetic science fiction writers of all time. In addition to his short stories, he has written plays, novels, poetry, and the script for the 1956 film version of *Moby Dick*. He lives in Los Angeles.

MARTHA SOUKUP has written science fiction and fantasy for adults—winning a Nebula

About the Authors

Award—as well as for kids, in *A Nightmare's Dozen, Bruce Coville's Book of Aliens II*, and other anthologies. She lives in San Francisco. Her cats live next door.

WILLIAM SLEATOR is the author of several award-winning books, including *The Spirit House* and *Strange Attractors*. He also composes music, and has worked as a pianist and ballet composer for the Royal Ballet School and the Boston Ballet. He now writes full-time, and divides his time between Boston and Bangkok, Thailand.

NINA KIRIKI HOFFMAN's short fiction has appeared in many magazines and anthologies, including several in this series. Her novel *The Thread that Binds the Bones* won a Bram Stoker award for first novel. She lives with many cats and has a witchball in her backyard.

JOHN PIERARD has illustrated all the books in this series, as well as the *My Teacher Is an Alien* quartet, the popular *My Babysitter Is a Vampire* series, and stories in *Isaac Asimov's Science Fiction Magazine*. He lives in New York City.

Photo: Jules

BRUCE COVILLE was born and raised in a rural area of central New York, where he spent his youth dodging cows and chores, and letting his imagination get out of hand. He first fell under the spell of writing when he was in sixth grade and his teacher gave the class an extended period of time to work on a short story.

Sixteen years later—after stints as a toymaker, a gravedigger, and an elementary school teacher—he published *The Foolish Giant*, a picture book illustrated by his wife and frequent collaborator, Katherine Coville. Since then Bruce has published more than fifty books for young readers, including the popular *My Teacher Is an Alien* series. He has long been fascinated by the art and science of fear, and thinks that making people's spines tingle is a useful and interesting thing to do. He is very happy to be considered a scary guy.

These days Bruce and Katherine live in an old brick house in Syracuse with their youngest child, Adam; their cats Spike, Thunder, and Ozma; and the Mighty Thor, an exceedingly exuberant Norwegian elkhound.